I0748135

THE EMBER ISLES
BLOOD MAGIC
BOOK FOUR

JT LAWRENCE

FIRE FINCH

FIRE FINCH

 Created with Vellum

About the Author
JT LAWRENCE

JT Lawrence is a USA Today bestselling author
of 30+ books, and a Kindle Unlimited All-Star. Mother to a
menagerie of chaos, voracious reader, gin fan, and urban
farmer.

Stay up all night
with USA Today bestselling author
JT Lawrence.

www.jt-lawrence.com

amazon.com/author/jtlawrence

tiktok.com/@stay_up_allnite

instagram.com/authorjtlawrence

facebook.com/JanitaTLawrence

x.com/stay_up_allnite

bookbub.com/authors/jt-lawrence

pinterest.com/stay_up_all_night

linkedin.com/in/janita-thiele-lawrence-56533610

SPECIAL THANKS

Immense gratitude to my readers
whose loyalty, support, and generous reviews
give me the courage to face the blank page
over and over again.

I wouldn't be able to do this without you.

I hope you enjoy this new magical adventure!

- Janita (JT Lawrence)

THE EMBER ISLES

BLOOD MAGIC BOOK 4

CHAPTER I

A HALF-KNITTED SAILBOAT

Morgan and I stood at the front of the Moonlit Chapel grounds and stared each other down.

"What do you mean?" I asked, her Scorpion captain's badge flashing in the morning sun. "What was Darick arrested for?"

She frowned and pursed her lips, as if she didn't know how to tell me.

"Spit it out, Morgan!" I said, a little louder than intended. I immediately regretted my grouchiness toward my best friend, but in my defense, it had been a long few days and I wasn't in the mood to stand around a creepy chapel that I had seen more than enough of, waiting for her to find the right phrasing. My skin was scorched, my bones were tired, and my brain was all kinds of fried. Still, Morgan hesitated, looking down and nudging the rock at her feet. She finally looked up, and her eyes flashed at me.

"Attempted murder," she said.

Then it was my turn to be lost for words. I opened my mouth and blinked at the sky, then at our surroundings: the cops milling around, the emergency vehicles crowding the narrow gray road. The ground was carpeted in dead leaves, the scene all wrapped up in yellow police tape.

"Not possible," I said.

Morgan crossed her arms and sighed. "I know it must be difficult to hear. I mean, it's clear that you two are—"

"It's not that," I said. "I'm telling you right now he's not—"

I was going to say *"not a killer,"* but I had seen Darick in action, and he was by far the most efficient assassin I had ever witnessed. I remembered, clear as day, the moment he brought out his gun with such an elegant and practiced movement, and put a bullet through the skull of one of the vampires who had attacked me outside *Cucina Or'Capone.* The vampire had knocked me out and was dragging me into a car when I woke up and saw Darick appear, out of nowhere. Who knows where the vampire would have taken me, or what he would have done to me? That was the first time Darick saved my life, even though I gave him a hard time about it. I told him to get lost, that I didn't need a superhero stalker, but he had other ideas.

"Attempted murder of whom?" I asked.

Someone evil, someone who had it coming. A criminal? A vampire? A Neo-Nazi orc?

"A sweet little old lady," Morgan said.

I almost laughed. "You're kidding."

"Not kidding," she said, and she did that thing she's so good at. Staring without blinking. "There's a very reliable witness."

Something wasn't adding up. My mind was whirring like an exercise wheel in the Guinea Pig Olympics. "Who's the old lady?"

"A patient at Silver Wing."

That's the hospital Hettie Frost was being treated at. Hettie Frost was a little old lady.

"Hang on," I said. "Was it Hettie Frost?"

"I don't know. Who is Hettie Frost?"

"The StarDust Coven witch who was buried alive."

"I don't know. I haven't seen the file. I was just eavesdropping at the watercooler. Detective Musubarin's on the case."

Hot dread tarred my insides. "Of course he is."

Morgan narrowed her eyes at me, and I felt suddenly uncomfortable under her scrutiny. "Listen, how well do you know this guy?"

"I know all I need to know about him. I wouldn't be alive if it wasn't for Darick, and neither would Gizmo."

"You know his last name?" she asked.

"Last names are overrated," I said. I did perfectly well with my Copperfield-appointed orphan surname, thank you very much.

"Do you know where he lives?" she asked. "Where he comes from? Family history?"

I shook my head. "No. Why does that matter?"

She kept her arms crossed and drummed her fingers. "How long have you known him?"

"A week," I fibbed. More like five days.

"So this totally random guy shows up in your life out of the blue and next thing he's living with you—"

"He's not living with me," I said.

"—And trying to murder pocket grannies in hospitals."

"He wasn't trying to murder her. Believe me, I've seen him in action. If Darick wanted someone dead, they'd be dead."

"You are not helping his case."

"That's probably true."

"That pocket granny was under police protection. Police protection that *you* asked for. He put some kind of sleeping spell on the guard and went in for the kill."

"The kill?" I said. "Since when do you jump to conclusions?"

"It's my job to jump to conclusions," she said.

"I know why he was there," I said. "I was the one who sent him."

Morgan angled her face at me. "What now?"

"When the witch hunter was at large, Hettie Frost was the only person who could tell us who the killer was. But after the trauma she was in some kind of coma—or trance—and she couldn't speak. Ophelia was out of control. She killed two coven members in one day. I had to stop her."

I couldn't help picturing them, then. Fidelis Wolfmoon, drowned in her bathtub, her baby grandson's jersey lying abandoned in her living room, a half-knitted sailboat on the front. And the grumpy old hag, Hazel Shackleton—may she rest in peace—who had run out of luck at the Great Oaks Medieval Fair in Brimware Grove, her limp body hanging from a noose above the sacred *Gallanrock*.

"I was out of options," I said. "Ophelia was going to kill Crowe, and the rest of the coven, and Hettie was the only one who knew who her attacker was. I sent Darick to Silver Wing to get an answer out of her."

"You sent Darick? Why? Is he some kind of granny whisperer?"

"He's a mage," I said. "A healer. I thought that if he could get her well enough to talk, she'd be able to tell us who the killer was."

"The machines in Frost's ward were going bonkers," said Morgan. "That's what alerted the nurse. She saw the unconscious cop at the door and barged in. Darick had his hands wrapped around Frost's throat."

"That's how he does his ... healing magic," I said. I had to admit, it sounded like bull, even to me.

Morgan's eyebrows shot up. "Healing by strangulation? That's a pretty unique talent to have."

"Ha," I said. "I meant he heals with his hands."

I could see that Morgan was not convinced.

"I'm not convinced," she said. "I mean, of course I believe you. It's *you*. But I don't know about this guy."

"Darick," I said.

"Darick. I mean, I know love can make you—"

"Whoa!" I said, taking a step back. A brittle stick snapped under my bonfire-disfigured boots. "Who said anything about love?"

I don't fall in love. Never have, never will. Way too much at stake. I know what happens when you love people. It makes you vulnerable.

"You forget," said Morgan, "that I'm a detective. And I know you better than anyone else. And when we talk about Darick you have stars in your eyes that I've never seen before."

"I don't!" I said, but I knew it was true.

"I just hope he's as worthy as you think he is," she said. "Because there's something about him that I don't trust."

"He can be infuriating sometimes," I admitted, remembering the time he had posed as an Uber driver and kidnapped me from outside an overpriced cocktail bar and driven me home. "And stubborn. And reckless."

"Hmm," said Morgan. "So you have a lot in common, then."

Morgan uncrossed her arms and sighed, signaling that the conversation was over. Her car keys dangled in her hand.

"I've got to get to the station," she said. "Process the Knox case. I'd invite you to come along to see your boyfriend—"

"He's not my boyfriend," I said.

"—But Musubarin will be at HQ, and if he sees you I'm pretty sure that he'll throw you in a cell with Ophelia."

I shuddered.

"He knows how to hold a grudge," I said. "I mean, it's been, what? At least twelve hours since I kicked him in the balls."

"Memory like an elephant," said Morgan, and gave me a skewed smile.

I laughed, and I felt some of the prior tension dissipate. She waved goodbye and turned, picking her way along the narrow path, towards her Scorpion-issued SUV. I watched as she started the car and drove away.

Bron, still hexed in his raven form, swooped down and perched on my shoulder, shaking his black wings in my ear. My trench coat protected my skin from his sharp claws.

"Come on, Kresnik," I said, following Morgan's footsteps towards my motorbike. "We've got an old friend to see."

CHAPTER 2
DRESDEN DRIVE

Abarim Manor, at 44 Dresden Drive, Westcliff, was exactly as I remembered it, except that the invisible sinister smog of Contagious Magic had disappeared. As I accelerated up the long driveway, petals from the Iceberg roses whirled in the air and floated down to the expertly laid paving stones below. I parked under the ancient oak and began to make my way up to the house. Again, I thought that it felt like a good, sturdy house. Well cared for, but not ridiculously manicured. Expensive, but not flashy. The solid structure and tasteful design whispered *"old money"*, as did the interior furnishings. Willard, the butler, seemed genuinely happy to see me. He smiled and took my hands in his, and said, "Welcome, Ms. Knight. Welcome. Do come in."

The first time I visited, when Blimeax Abarim's butler had hired me to help his employer, Willard was a nervous man, jumpy and afraid, stretched to his limit by Abarim's suffering. He looked so different now. It had only been a few days, but Willard looked like he had gone on a tropical island cruise. His face had some color in it; his eyes were rested and sparkling. He still wore his severe black suit, but his face was kind and relaxed whereas before it was bleached by fear. I could actually see his silver-gray eyebrows now; before they had just blended into his stark white face.

"You look well," I said, and he nodded.

"I feel well," he said, and bowed. I don't think I'll ever get used to being bowed to, but I appreciated the gesture nonetheless. "All thanks to you."

The butler led me up the generous steps and through the entrance hall, where the air was cool. The exotic orchids had been replaced by some freshly cut irises, which I was sure were from the vast garden. The silver antiques gave me the idea that they were trying to outshine each other.

"Mister Abarim is in his study."

I felt a little chilled when he said that, because what I remembered from Abarim's study was the pile of children's fairy tale books, and the one that still gave me nightmares, *The Dream Drinker*. Blimaex had given the old book to me as a rather poignant gift after I had helped him escape the far-reaching magical clutches of his evil brother. I had squeezed it onto my overloaded bookshelf and not taken it out again. Some children's stories are more frightening than adult fiction, and I don't need more nightmare fuel.

We reached Blimaex's study and Willard cleared his throat to announce our arrival, but the old wizard was so deeply entrenched in whatever he was studying that he didn't notice our shadows darkening his door.

Willard put on his very best butler face and tried again, and this time Abarim looked up past his half-moon bifocals and his face lit up. He stood with open arms.

"Ms. Knight," he said. "I was so pleased to receive your request for a meeting."

He moved towards me, his purple astronomy-print robe swaying as he walked. I thought he might hug me, but instead he patted me on the shoulder. "Good to see you, good to see you."

Willard settled us on the couches near the cold fireplace with rooibos tea and some rather insipid English biscuits, which I wolfed down because I couldn't remember the last time I had eaten.

"I WAS glad to hear I may be of assistance to you," said Blimaex. "Tell me what is on your mind."

I dusted the crumbs from my fingers and set down my empty teacup, taking care not to break the fragile thing painted with rose apples and gold. The painting on the delicate porcelain moved as I looked at it; from apple, to seeds, to bloom, and back to apple.

"A friend of mine is in trouble," I said. "He needs a lawyer. And I've heard that you're the best defense attorney in the city."

Abarim's eyebrows arched. "I can assure you that is not true."

"You're the perfect person for the job," I said. "I know it."

The old wizard sighed, took off his specs, and held them in his lap. "I haven't practiced criminal law in thirty years. Not since I was elected to the Council."

"The law hasn't changed very much," I said. I was guessing, of course. I had barely been alive for thirty years, and what I knew about the Realm's legal system would tempt a judge to binge-drink. Still, I knew I was onto something, because Abarim nodded slowly and his lips sloped downwards in agreement.

"You have a point," he said. He looked quite stately then, in his purple wizard's cloak, surrounded by a backdrop of handsome, neatly shelved books. A large hardcover notebook rested on the coffee table before him, the corners of which were edged in pewter.

Willard came back to clear the tray, and Blimaex asked the butler to bring him his staff. Willard bowed and reversed out of the room, a talent I found quite impressive. If it had been me, those dainty cups and saucers would be lying shattered on the hardwood floor.

He returned with the wizard's staff, styled like a simple African *knobkerrie*. It was only when you looked closely that you saw gold sparks flecking the wood's grain. Blimaex held it up and cleared the air in front of him, then looked at me pointedly.

"Name?" he said.

"Darick," I said, and cursed myself for the second time that morning for not knowing Darick's surname. Abarim waited for it, then realized it was not forthcoming.

"Darick," he said, and swept the staff between us again. The large book on the coffee table before him flicked open of its own accord and the pages swiftly turned themselves, perfuming the air with a glorious old book smell. Leaves of notes scribbled in black, blue, and purple ink, textured with tea stains and crumbs. The pages turned until they stopped on a new blank page. Abarim looked expectantly at the cream paper.

We waited, staring at the empty page, and then the writing began to appear.

CHAPTER 3
INVISIBLE INK

When I was a little girl, my father taught me how to do "spy writing" with invisible ink. We picked a lemon from our burgeoning tree in the courtyard and squeezed the juice into an old, chipped saucer the color of bone. Then, with a fine paintbrush, we wrote secret messages on our pieces of crisp white paper and let them dry in the sun. Then Dad gave me his lighter—the one he used to light the fire on winter nights—and an old stump of a candle. He taught me how to hold the citrus-scented paper just the right distance away from the flame. Too close, and the paper would burst into flames, destroying the message. Too far, and the message would remain invisible.

The very first time Dad showed me the trick I was sure it was magic, but he explained the science behind it. The lemon juice is a weak acid, which softens the fibers in the paper. Adding heat forces some of the chemical bonds to break down in the dried juice and some carbon is cut loose, and oxidation occurs.

Like magic, I said, and he smiled. I didn't really see the difference. Hanging inside Ferra's office, just outside her high-tech laboratory at the *Copper Cog & Ale*, is a framed Arthur C. Clarke quote embroidered in copper thread: *Any sufficiently advanced technology is indistinguishable from magic.*

JUST LIKE MY invisible ink darkened into letters and drawings, so did the pages of Blimaex Abarim's pewter-edged notebook, although his version was being written before our eyes. It was an eccentric but uniform handwriting, and splatters of ink appeared as the information about Darick's case was revealed. An illustration appeared, too, in the top left hand corner. A mug shot. And then I read his name—albeit upside down—for the first time: *DARICK NOBLE.*

I breathed in deeply, as if I was absorbing his name, and I felt comforted by it. I finally knew his whole name. Also, "*Darick*" may sound distinctly vampiric, but "*Noble*" was not a common family name for a bloodsucker.

Abarim put his spectacles back on and began to study the page. I strained my neck, caught between trying to see what else was being written and not wanting to appear nosy. The wizard let out soft murmurings of interest. *Uh-huh,* he said. *Mm-hm. I see.*

Suddenly, he stopped dead. It was only for a second, for the span of a held breath, while he blinked hard and then quickly wiped something away, as if he had noticed a stray hair or dead ant. The offending information was swept off the page, and then his breathing and muttering returned to normal.

What? I wanted to say. *What is it?* I was desperate to know.

"Right!" said the wizard, slamming the book shut and making me jolt in my chair. "I think I have a handle on the case."

"You do?"

"Open and shut, as they say."

I looked at the book and thought if Qwynkle were here, he'd appreciate the pun. Goblins love their puns, and treacherous gangster goblins were no exception.

"The Scorpions' case is weak, at best. Honestly, I would expect more from them."

"It's the new detective there," I said. "Tilexon Musubarin."

Abarim looked at me sharply. "A wizard?" he said. "On the squad?"

I nodded.

"That's highly irregular."

"That's what I thought, too. But no one argues with the Council, right?"

"I beg your pardon?"

"Tilexon was a Council appointment."

"That can't be right," he said. "That doesn't sound appropriate at all."

"Mister Abarim," I said. "May I ask ... you were on the Council for thirty years, before you fell ill? Willard said you were looking forward to getting back to work."

Blimaex frowned. "Yes," he said, and stood up. He ambled towards the window. "I alerted the Council to my restored health, but they decided they were no longer in need of my services."

I frowned. "But that's not how it works."

Council wizards were never fired, demoted, or retrenched. They were the purest of heart in the Realm, the wisest and the most powerful. Once a wizard was elected to Council he remained on the Council till his dying day.

"They were no longer in need of your services?" I said. "That's—"

I was going to say, *"that's ridiculous"*, but thought better of it. The walls had ears and eyes, even here in the relative safety of Abarim Manor.

"That doesn't make any sense," I said. "Have they replaced you?"

Abarim shook his head. "An eleven-member Council?" I said.

That was unprecedented. If nothing else, they needed the manpower. I had been trying to get hold of them for days but they never answered any of my messages. When I tried to call in, no-one answered. And now, with the Hammerskin unrest ...

"I thought it was perhaps because of my brother," Blimaex said. "When Slyden slid into the Dark Arts it was a stain on the whole family. The election committee was willing to overlook it, as long as my personal record was sparkling. But when Slyden joined forces with the Silvano Clan, well ... I don't think any magical family can come back from that."

Abarim had a point, but it was hardly fair or right. We looked at each other for a while, his words hanging in the air like cigarette smoke.

"Darick's case," I said. "You think it's open and shut?"

"All they have is a witness."

"Isn't that enough?" I asked. "Morgan—she's the captain of the Scorpions—said she's an extremely reliable witness. She's been a nurse at Silver Wing for years. Hardworking, honest."

"I'll let you in on a little trick of the trade," said Abarim. "There's no such thing as a reliable witness."

"What do you mean?"

"Even the most accurate eyewitness accounts are fraught with inconsistencies and mis-remembered details."

"I don't understand."

"We're human. We have baggage. Our glasses are tinted with who we are and what we've seen. Add to that the volatility of our memories and how quickly they decay, and how our brains automatically paint in the missing details, often incorrectly, and you'll see very quickly that there is no such thing as a reliable witness."

I felt as if Blimaex had handed me a key. Not necessarily to unlock Darick's case, but to use in my future investigations. I seemed to have the knack of knowing when people were lying to me, and that served me well in my line of work. But what I often forgot was that people may be well-intentioned, and telling the truth, but it was their experience, and their truth. I had no doubt that the nurse really did believe Darick was trying to kill her patient, but that didn't make her testimony any less flawed.

"So that's what you'll argue in court?" I said, and then realized I was way ahead of myself. The man hadn't yet agreed to defend Darick. I felt a blush burn my cheeks.

"I'm hoping it won't get that far," said the wizard, stroking his beard thoughtfully. "I think we may be able to get it thrown out before wasting a judge's time."

"So, you'll take the case?" I asked. Usually people ask me that question, so it felt strange to be on the other side of the equation.

Blimaex looked surprised by my question. "Of course I'll take the case!"

"I don't want you to feel obligated," I said, which was only a half-truth. I didn't mind the old man feeling obligated if it meant he'd get Darick out of jail.

"I *do* feel obligated," he said, then winked at me. "But that's not the reason I'm taking the case."

I looked up at him.

"You say this man is innocent, correct?"

"Correct," I said.

"Well, that is enough for me."

CHAPTER 4
DRAGON'S MAW

I sped over to Scorpion HQ, my motorbike alive beneath me, the blue sky overhead beaming brightly with my renewed hope. We were going to get Darick out of jail. We were going to find a way to reverse Bron's hex. We were going to thwart the vampires' audacious plans to take over the Realm. It was not without satisfaction that I remembered my chemical bomb blowing up the Vampire Venom lab—and a couple of Hammerskins for luck—and I was happy to be the thorn in Acheron Baldassare's side.

I knew Morgan warned me to stay away from the station because of that annoying wizard with the shiny new detective badge, but I needed to see Darick. I wanted him to feel the new hope that I felt strumming in my chest. It would make his confinement bearable, I thought, if he knew that one of the most respected lawyers in the country was on his side, and that he had me in his corner, ready to fight for his freedom. Energy surged through me. It was a nice change from the chronic exhaustion I had been plagued by.

It's amazing what a bike ride and a little hope can do.

Around ten minutes before I reached the building, I noticed some pedestrians acting in an odd way, and some cars driving recklessly, as if they were trying to get away from something. A handful of the people looked panicked, distraught, but I couldn't tell what the problem was. A fire? I didn't see any smoke, or smell anything burning. An armed robbery, perhaps? Jozi is cowboy country, after all. My instincts told me to take a turn towards the excitement, but I ignored it. I wanted to stay out of trouble, for once. Just for long enough to get my message through to Darick.

I arrived at the Scorpion headquarters and, instead of buzzing Morgan like I would usually do, I asked the officer at the reception desk to call Detective Tilexon Musubarin. He tried his office, but it just rang.

"Sorry," the fresh-faced officer said. "He's not in. Can I take a message?"

"When the cat's away," said Morgan, from her desk.

"Any idea how long the cat will be away for?" I asked.

"Not sure. I think he's in a management meeting."

"A management meeting?" I asked. "Without you?"

Morgan shrugged. "I'm getting used to it. There's a silver lining to being invisible. It means more time to get work done."

"Like trying to solve the V-Cult case," I said.

She nodded, a grim look on her face. "Like trying to solve the V-Cult case," she agreed.

"Which reminds me," I said. "I have something for you."

"Goddess," Morgan said, rubbing her forehead. I wasn't sure if she was cursing or complimenting me. "Please let it be a bottle of blitz."

"Ah, sorry." I shrugged. "Not a bottle of blitz."

It wasn't alcohol, but if it was, it would be a sweet rosé. I pulled Liz Durison's little black book from my pocket.

"Remember this?" I said. "Your neighbor's little black book."

"Of course I remember it," Morgan said. "It's how we tracked down Chuck Winnow."

I remembered losing control of my magic at Winnow's house. I had been so frustrated that our lead hadn't taken us to the V-Cult killer that my magic just flew out of me and tornadoed his office. It wasn't the most terrible thing that could have happened though, because it meant we found that candid shot of me in his desk drawer, and it had confirmed our worst suspicions. Suffice to say, it was no coincidence that every single victim who the vamp cult drained and branded just happened to look very much like me. Who knew so many doppelgängers existed? Walking around, going to work and dinners and art galleries without a clue that they were pretty much carbon copies of each other.

If only they were real clones, I thought. Able to investigate paranormal enquiries and locate stolen magical items and just generally kick vampire butt. I would be able to finally solve all the cases on my list. I would be able to buy groceries and have lunch with Morgan and have a life. And then I remembered, clones or not, they were lying dead on the cold steel sliding drawers in the fridges in the city morgue, stitched up with the coroner's awful blue nylon. Or maybe they were already buried in the cold earth, or burnt to nothing in the frightening dragon's maw of the crematorium. Either way, they were gone, and I was the last one left. And as the ghost of Liz Durison liked to remind me, between her gulps of sweet pink wine, I owed it to them to find the killers.

Morgan snapped her fingers in front of my face, rudely forcing me out of my reverie.

"Jax," she said. "Are you okay?"

"Yes?" I answered.

Was I okay? I wasn't sure.

"When last did you eat?" she asked, sounding like Ferra. "When last did you sleep?"

Again, I wasn't sure. My life had become a blur of fire and blood and magic.

"You went all hazy there for a moment," said Morgan. "And pale. Come," she said, showing me a chair piled high with paperwork that she quickly swept onto the floor. "Come and sit down."

I shook my head, blinking. "No, really. I'm fine."

She rummaged in her handbag and threw me a protein bar. I took it gratefully. It's not easy to think sometimes, when your head is crowded with ghosts and other unwelcome creatures. But I had to get on with it and get out of there. I passed Durison's book to Morgan.

"It's yours," I said. "I hope you find something useful in it."

Morgan took it from me and grinned. "Thank you!"

She spent some time running her fingers over the cover, then opened it at a random place.

"Wow," she said, blowing a strand of hair out of her face. "I would never have guessed."

"Would never have guess what?" I asked. "That she had so many lovers?"

"It makes me feel kind of inadequate," said Morgan.

I laughed. "Don't get me started."

"I know, right?"

"And she looked so vanilla from the outside," I said. "Vanilla everything."

"Just goes to show you. You think you know someone." Morgan gave me a meaningful look, and I knew what she meant. You see what you want to see. She had seen Durison as a friendly neighbor who she felt okay leaving her kids with if she had an emergency call. It's not that the appearance was wrong; it was just simplistic. And humans are far from being simple beings. Morgan wanted me to see past the idea I had of Darick and look for his true nature, his complications. It was difficult for me, because when I thought of him all I saw was a broad-shouldered, powerfully-built superhero with a tendency to save lives in general, and mine in particular. When I was with him I felt a heady combination of safety in his arms, and an intense desire to go deeper into his body.

I knew what Morgan was saying, but I was too far gone, like when you know you should stop drinking after the third whisky but some new hunger kicks in, a wild craving for the warmth of it, and the release, and you accept the next drink, even though you know it won't be good for you. You think, I know there'll be price to pay, but I will pay for it tomorrow. It's the borrowed happiness that comes before the hangover.

Morgan's neck snapped up from reading the *Flint* book. "Wanna grab lunch?"

Usually my answer to lunch would be unhesitatingly affirmative, but I had to sneak in a quick visit to Darick before Musubarin came back. Before I had time to answer Morgan, there was a yell of fright from the open-plan sergeants' desks outside her office. We frowned at each other and Morgan automatically felt for her gun. She didn't pull it; she just wanted to know it was there.

"Stay here," she said to me, and when I ignored her and followed, she stopped and turned, and I almost bumped into her. "I mean it," she said, so I put my hands up in surrender and widened my eyes. "Okay!" I whispered.

Morgan made her way towards the origin of the scream, and I stood in the doorway, listening hard.

"It's bad," said a quavering voice. "It's really bad, Captain. I don't know if—"

"Move over," ordered Morgan, in a stern voice. "Let me see ... what the—?"

And then her voice trailed off.

CHAPTER 5

A CLANG OF A TIN CUP

I was straining to hear, but Morgan wasn't talking. There were just the recorded voices and panicked screams of the video they were watching. What was it? A terrorist attack in the US? A beheading in Belarus? And then I remembered the panicked pedestrians I had seen on my way there; and the odd way the cars were driving. They had been getting away from something. Something that was right on our doorstep. I wanted Morgan to come back into the office and tell me what had happened, but then I had another idea. I could use the distraction to my advantage.

When Morgan had swept the pile of paperwork to the floor, I had noticed a Scorpion-branded legal page impressed with neat blue ballpoint pen handwriting. I hadn't been able to read it as it floated to the floor, but I could tell it was new by the crispness of the sheet. I quickly searched for it, and found it underneath Morgan's desk. It lay on the floor along with old receipts for coffee, and copies of various files and records with photos that reminded me of Blimaex Abarim's magical notebook, and the artful illustration of Darick's mugshot.

It also made me wonder what Abarim had seen in that book that made his face contract; the detail that he had swept off the page with the back of his hand and pretended had never existed.

I looked at the A4 paper being softened and warped in my clammy palm, and skimmed the words that textured it. It was dated that morning, and written by the head nurse at Silver Wing Medical Center. It was the testimony of the "reliable witness."

The nurse had entered the police-secured ward of Hettie Frost and found an unknown male at her bedside, his hands wrapped around her throat. She had pressed the panic button, sounding the alarm, and the hospital's security guards had hurried to assist. Darick had not fought them, had not tried to run. He had not acted guilty in any way, but he had also not said anything in his defense.

The nurse's name was Kim Smith, a *Jane Doe* name if I'd ever heard one. The kind they give to dead prostitutes who have no friends or family come to identify their lonely corpses. The kind who could have had a better life, if only they hadn't been hurt by their uncles or bullied at school, or stripped bare emotionally by the verbal barbs of their abusive alcoholic mothers. But this Kim Smith had made something of her life, despite her name, which made me want to like her.

I took Kim Smith's signed witness statement and folded it in a hurry, then slipped it into my trench coat's inner pocket.

The guilt stung me a bit, but only for a second. Growing up on the cold streets of Jo'burg and hanging out with the other Feral kids taught me a lot, and one of the most important lessons was *sometimes you've gotta take what you've gotta take.*

Usually this applied to using the quick and dirty magic they schooled me in, to grab a cardigan here and a tenner there, just to get through the days that yawned before us. Stealing money to buy something unnecessary would have been wrong, they said. But staying alive was a different matter. And we always seemed to be on that blurry line, that edge of hunger and survival. We watched as some of our friends fell over that cliff. Bongi, who had fallen asleep thinking she was warm enough. Wandile, who had gone with the man who promised her a meal and come back with the spark snuffed out of her eyes. It was brutal to think about, but for many years it was our reality. It was how life worked.

It's a little different now, I thought, *but at the core of it, it's just as brutal.*

Every day was still a battle for survival. It was more comfortable. I had an apartment and a bed and a ghost who liked to do my laundry. But I still had the pangs from being an orphan, and I was still living on that knife's edge between life and death.

THE OFFICERS WERE CROWDED around the screen of the cop who had, minutes earlier, screamed at what she had seen. I wanted to see it, too, but I realized that this was probably the only gap I would get to see Darick, so I had to take it. I inched out of Morgan's office and darted towards the emergency stairs. I ran down the two flights I knew would take me to the SubT—the Scorpion HQ's subterranean holding cells. Usually I liked the idea that the lock-up was underground and impossible to escape from, but that's when I was thinking about evil orcs and goblin gang leaders. I had never before been friends with someone who was incarcerated down there; I automatically thought of all of them as deserving pond scum. But that was when Morgan was in charge. With Musubarin, things had changed. There was no telling who he'd lock up, innocent or guilty. Granted, he wasn't the Big Kahuna yet, but I knew, as well as Morgan did, that her days of being captain of the squad were numbered. She had accepted it, but I hadn't.

Wizard or not, Musubarin was a creep. I'd be stuck in one of the cells if I hadn't kicked Tilexon in the toolbox, and I'd be happy to do it again, if the situation called for it—you'd be surprised at how often a situation requires that kind of response.

The subterranean cells were dark and smelled of damp, and as I pressed myself up against the black-bricked wall something slithered over my hand and I almost yelled in fright. I waited, heart-in-throat, for my breathing to return to normal before moving forward. Water dripped.

The SubT cells were older than the Scorpion HQ building, and most of the city. They were originally built when the first gold miners came to town and needed a place to sling thieves and murderers in. Instead of abandoning the ore-poor shaft, they put some iron bars in and called it a jail. In the hundred-plus years it's been used, no one had ever broken out. There was nowhere to escape to. Every time Morgan considered getting it modernized, she looked at her desperate refurb budget and put it off for another time. It did its job and it didn't complain ... much. Sometimes, late at night, when she was burning the midnight oil trying to get on top of her caseload, Morgan would hear sounds from down there. Shifting sounds, or weeping. Sometimes it was the clang of a tin cup on the bars. She would pat her gun and go down there, and see that the cells were empty.

CHAPTER 6

THE MORE INTIMATE, THE MORE DANGEROUS

Around the corner, yellow light cascaded from a bare bulb hanging from the rock ceiling.

"Darick?" I whispered, my pulse thudding in my ears. I moved, cautiously, to the first cell. It, like the others, was enclosed with black, rusted bars. My eyes were still adjusting to the dim light so I had to peer in. It was a mistake. A gray-skinned goblin slammed himself against the bars, giving me such a scare I couldn't help but jump backwards and shout in fright. He stuck his greasy arm out at me, trying to grab my hair with fingers that were black and dripping with slime—at least, I hoped it was slime—and spoke to me through his brown needle-like teeth.

"Pretty-y-y-y-y," he said, gnashing his jaws at me as if he thought I was his dinner. I felt a sting on my scalp, and I saw in his palm that he had managed to get a strand of my hair. He leered and held it to his chest.

"Give it back," I said, but the creature just laughed.

It was dangerous, having a part of yourself, your body, out in the dark side of the Realm. Your hair, or nail clippings, or a piece of clothing—the more intimate, the more dangerous—could be used for contagious magic. I had seen the effects of Contagious Magic firsthand, when Slyden Abarim used it to attack his brother. Blimaex had been tortured for days before he had almost died.

"Give it back," I said again, and the goblin's eyes narrowed at me, and he hissed, spraying me with his sour saliva. I unclipped my wand and held it out between us, ready to take back what was mine. "Listen here, Needle-Teeth. You're going to give me my hair back right now or I'm going to *Rumpis* your slimy ass."

The goblin hissed at me again.

"Last chance, gremlin," I said, pointing my wand at the space between his eyes.

Of course, I couldn't use a destruction spell on him, not down here. I couldn't risk blowing the bars open and destroying Scorpion property. I was in enough trouble as it was. Instead, I just sent a concentrated fire spell towards the ribbon of my hair he held triumphantly in his hand.

"Ignem Exquiris!" I said, and sent a small but potent fireball into his hand. I heard it sizzle against his snail-skin as it hit, and he cried out. The disgusting smell of burnt hair and seared goblin flesh filled my nostrils. *Good.*

The goblin looked at his empty palm and shrieked in anger, then launched himself at me again, slamming himself up against the bars just as I jumped away from them. I was tempted to sling one last spell, just to teach the miscreant a lesson, but I held back. I was down there for a reason, and I was running out of time. For all I knew, Musubarin was already back at his desk. I lowered my wand and clipped it to my belt.

"Jax?" called the voice I'd been missing; the voice to quieten all voices. My heart was hammering and I wished it would calm down so that I could take in the full effect.

"Jax?"

It was coming from the last cell in the row. I jogged towards it.

"Darick," I said. "I'm so sorry."

He stood behind the dark steel paling. His face was white, but he didn't look hurt.

"You're sorry?" he said.

"I'm the one who asked you to go to Hettie Frost. You wouldn't have been arrested if it weren't for me. You wouldn't be down here in this—"

"Don't worry about that," Darick said. "You have no idea how happy I am to see you."

"I'm going to fix it, though. I have a plan."

Darick grinned. "You're not planning on breaking me out of here, are you?"

"That's Plan B."

He put his hands on the bars, wrapping his fingers around them. "I wasn't hurting her," he said. "Frost. I was trying to heal her."

"I know, I know."

"Just in case you needed to hear it from me. I wasn't hurting her."

"Darick," I said, looking into his eyes. "I know."

He paused. "But there are things that you … don't know," he said.

"So people keep telling me."

Lou, for one, who hadn't thought it necessary to tell me that she just happened to be a djinni, or about her samurai skills, which were on fleek.

"Care to fill me in, then?"

"I will. But not now," he said. "Not here."

I'd thought my days of being infuriated by Darick were over, but I was wrong.

"I've hired a lawyer for you," I said. "He's already on the case. He thinks you'll be out of here in no time."

"Thank the Void," said Darick, nodding in the direction of the grayskin. "That goblin's singing is the worst."

"Worse than mine?" I asked.

A few days before, Darick had heard me belting out a song in the shower when I thought I was home alone. Most people would go running for the hills when exposed to that kind of ear-torture, but Darick had stayed, and passed me a towel.

"Maybe not worse than yours," he said. "But ... he's not as pretty."

We smiled at each other, and it broke the tension, although a new kind of tightness seemed to coalesce between us as we remembered that day: the steam in the air, the water droplets on warm skin, the dropped towel, the almost-kiss.

"If you can get hold of my phone up there," he pointed to the roof of his subterranean cell. "You'll find my bank details saved under the contact name Ducats. The numbers are reversed."

"How do you know I won't just take your money and go shoe shopping?"

Darick looked down at my melted boots. "You're welcome to."

"I was kidding."

"I wasn't," he said. "And buy yourself some groceries while you're at it."

"Now you're starting to sound bossy," I said.

He ignored me. "And some food for Gizmo. Real food. Not pentacle pretzels."

"I thought he was a vegetarian," I said, and Darick began to laugh. After a while, I joined in.

Then we both stopped smiling. I wanted to hold his hand through the bars but I didn't reach out for him, I don't know why.

"You still haven't told me what happened to you guys," I said. "Where you had to go to get Gizmo back. What you had to do. Why you were in such bad shape, and why Gizmo smelled of smoke."

Darick sighed and rubbed his face. "Yes."

"Let me guess," I said, crossing my arms over my chest. "Not now?"

"No," he said. "Now is good. I would have told you earlier if I could have. There's something you need to know."

CHAPTER 7
ONE HUNDRED GOLD POINTS

"I knew how much you were missing Gizmo," he said. "So I went to find him. I snapped off a leaf from the plant in your kitchen and asked Salty if she could help me portal to whatever was left of the volcano pocket realm."

"You're crazy," I said.

"I thought that if Gizmo wasn't able to find his way home, then he must be trapped somewhere. Also, I wanted to know what had become of that realm. The fact that the HighFire Crown was there somewhere meant that it could prop up the Silvanos' magic, and the realm would stabilize again. We saw it burning and crumbling, but by the time I went back to the volcano it was restored."

"Restored?"

"It was active, but stable, and there was no longer that silver shimmer in the air. And, more than that, there was a whole island around it, with vegetation and animals, and birds."

"I don't understand."

"The volcano swallowed that crown, right? And that gave it all this magical power to grow and proliferate."

"Like the plant in my kitchen," I said. "So if the volcano has the crown, that's okay? Because the Silvano Clan don't have it?"

Darick rubbed his face again. "That's what I thought. My plan was to find Gizmo and get out of there. But when I found him, he was sick. I could feel his ribs when I held him. He had been trying to get into the volcano the whole time, trying to find the crown. He knew it was in there. I had the feeling that he wouldn't leave the island without it."

My heart contracted. Poor Gizmo.

"So I realized I had to get the crown, if I wanted him to come home with me. I had the feeling he'd die trying to get in there. And he was right; leaving it on the island would be a mistake. It would be too dangerous."

"So you went into the volcano?"

"Most of it was uninhabitable, but there were some chambers that weren't burning. I figured the crown had to be in one of those if it was still in one piece. Gizmo and I worked as a team: he showed me the way, and I broke down the walls that had been keeping him out."

"You found the HighFire Crown," I said.

But they hadn't brought it back with them, so what had happened?

"The moment we located the crown, under a pile of lava rocks, the vampires showed themselves."

"Oh, *faex*," I said.

"They had been there all along, waiting for us to find it for them."

Anger flared up inside me, and my fingers began to tingle.

"Of course they were," I said.

"Gizmo fought bravely, even though he was tired and weak. I killed at least a dozen. But they just kept coming. Salty was still waiting at the portal, keeping it open for us. We needed to get out of the volcano and get back to her, but they weren't letting us go. Not with the crown."

"So you had to give it up," I said, the idea making me feel sick to my stomach.

He shook his head, and his expression was pained. "I didn't give it up," he said. "I would have rather died than given those vampires that crown. But I had played right into their hands."

"They took it from you."

"Yes," he said, swallowing his emotion. "That's why I need to go back."

"No," I said.

"They cannot have that crown," he said. "They cannot. It would mean the end of the Realm as we know it. I need to reverse the damage I've done."

"I'll come with you," I said. "I'll get you out of here and we'll both go."

"Unfortunately it's not as simple as that."

"What do you mean?"

"SaltySnap," he said, looking up in a way that made me think for a second that he was hiding something.

"What about her?"

"Salty wasn't at the portal when we went back to it. I thought she had become tired of waiting and decided to travel back without us, which was fine, because the gateway was open just enough for us to get through—"

"But now she's missing."

"Yes," he said, looking at the floor.

"Darick," I said. "Is there something you're not telling me?"

He stopped avoiding my eyes, then, and I felt the hot glare of them.

"Jax," he said. But then there were boots running down the stairs at the entrance of the cells and I backed up against the wall, praying nothing would scamper over me. I pressed myself up against the black bricks, under the cover of shadows, and held my breath. With any luck, it was just a meal delivery, and the orc doing the rounds would drop off the prisoner's lunches and leave without noticing me hiding behind him. But it turned out that Lady Luck was not in my subterranean corner, because the heavy footsteps belonged to Detective Musubarin, who strode in as if he owned the place.

I thought, *Just don't move, don't breathe, and he won't see you.* But I had forgotten, of course, that he was a wizard, and he felt my presence down there before he even reached Darick's cell. He stopped and sniffed the air, no doubt smelling the remnants of my singed hair. When he spoke, he sounded amused.

"Jacquelyn Denna Knight," he said, and I sighed and stepped out from the shelter of the dark.

"Detective," I said.

He had a splint over his nose, where I had broken it with my heel, and his bruised eyes lit up when he saw me. "Well. Isn't this convenient? In my pocket I have I warrant for your arrest—"

"Rubbish," I said.

"—and here you are, choosing a cell."

"You know I didn't do anything wrong," I said.

"Would you like the cell right next to your boyfriend?" he asked. "Or would you prefer the goblin as a neighbor?"

"You wanted to question me about the witch murders," I said. "And now you have not one, but three suspects under arrest."

"Oh," he said. "I know you didn't kill those witches. But there are other charges—"

"Trumped up charges," I said.

"Assault of a police officer," he said.

"I didn't have a choice," I said. "You were about to arrest me for a crime I didn't commit, and Isadora Crowe's life was in danger."

"And what kind of message would I be sending out, if I let you get off scot-free after assaulting—and slinging spells—at members of the Scorpion squad? No, Ms. Knight. That wouldn't do. I'm afraid you'll need to be punished."

"No," I said. No way was I languishing down there when the Realm was falling apart.

"No?" scowled the wizard detective. He opened and closed the right hand of his fist, as if he wanted to punch me, or hex me. I wasn't going to give him the chance.

"Leave her alone, Tilexon," said Darick.

The wizard spun around. "Shut up, Noble," he sneered. "You're in enough trouble, as it is."

"You know he's innocent," I said. "The only reason he's down here is because you wanted *me*."

"Ah," he said. "Maybe you are more intelligent than I gave you credit for. Either way, it worked beautifully, didn't it?"

His hand shot out at me before I could reflect the magic, and a blue ball of light hit my wrists, leaving a jangling pair of handcuffs behind. It happened so quickly my words deserted me, and I blinked at the cuffs disbelievingly.

"Take those off her right now," said Darick. He was a growling bear.

"You're in no position to tell me what to do," said the wizard, and moved towards me, wrenching my arm. I cried out in pain.

Darick threw himself at the bars and roared, and even I jumped in fright. A couple of the metal bars were bent. Musubarin took a moment to recover, but then cleared his throat. "My, my. This day is getting better and better." He unclipped his walkie-talkie from his belt and clicked a switch.

"Moose here. I'm in the SubT cells, do you copy?"

Some static came through, then someone picked up.

"Copy, Detective. Go ahead."

"I need some backup here down in the SubT. I caught a prisoner trying to escape. Noble."

"Copy that. Sending down support now."

"It's too dangerous to keep Noble here," said Musubarin. "Arrange for a transfer. Somewhere with maximum security."

"You can't do that!" I shouted. "He hasn't even stood trial yet!"

"And after that you can process the formal arrest of Jacquelyn Denna Knight. I have her in custody. She'll be in cell..." his eyes scanned the numbers carved into the rock above the bars. He looked at the number of the cell next to goblin. It said 2B. "She'll be in cell 2B."

"Copy that," said the cop on the other side.

"Jax! Run!" shouted Darick, but I didn't want to leave him down there. "Run!" he yelled again, and I did. I took flight up the rocky steps, trying my best not to fall and crack my skull open. It was tricky, with my wrists handcuffed, and the steps shrouded in dark. Plus my adrenaline had made me shaky. Musubarin was hot my heels and reached out to grab my foot just as I made it to the top of the steps, and he almost pulled me backwards, which would have made us both tumble down to the hard rock floor. As I felt myself lose my balance I shouted out *"Volas!"*. It gave me just enough lift to regain the traction I needed to scramble away from him and slam and bolt the door from the other side.

"Ignem exquiris!" I whispered. Using my wand as a blow-torch, I melted the metal of the door against the frame, sealing it. Tilexon starting bashing against heavy steel, but all he was going to get from his effort were bruised hands, which, I thought, would match his eyes quite nicely.

I RAN to the charges counter and yelled at the cop standing there, cleaning his fingernails with a paperclip.

"Moose needs you right away!"

He dropped the paperclip and his eyes lost their dreamy look. "What?"

"There's trouble down in SubT," I said. "Didn't you hear him on the two-way radio?"

The cop set his jaw and felt for his gun, then left his station at a pace, locking the stable door behind him. Not having to hide my cuffed wrists anymore, I brought them up to the counter and used it as leverage to jump over. I found the handcuffs key first, and unlocked the silver bracelets, dropping them on the floor. On second thoughts, I picked them up again and slipped them, along with the keys, into my trench coat pocket.

"Thanks, Moose." I said, under my breath.

"Never look a gift pony in the mouth," Ferra always says. I guess the dwarfs adapted the saying to suit their height limitations.

Next, I searched for Darick's personal effects, the belongings that had been taken from him when they brought him in. I found a clear plastic bag with his phone and his gun, and those went into my pocket, too. There was an identical resealable bag filled with dirty black fabric, and marked with HUX KRUQ. I figured it must belong to the detestable goblin down there. I quickly stood up and glanced left and right, to make sure no one was around the counter. I opened the packet. The stench was unbearable, and I quickly closed it again. I didn't know why, but I slid that into my pocket, too, and then hightailed it out of the Scorpion HQ building and jumped on my bike. I was starting to feel like I was in some kind of video game, collecting tokens. I imagined little gold points like coins above my head, rolling higher with each pocketed treasure. Handcuffs: two points; Gun: ten points; A particularly nasty gray-skinned goblin's old underwear: one hundred gold points. Or perhaps negative points, depending on what exactly turned out to be in the bag, and on which game we were playing.

CHAPTER 8
SPIKE

"What the hell just happened?" asked Morgan. Her voice sounded small over the speakers in my smart helmet. "Where are you?"

"Speeding away from HQ as fast as my bike will take me," I said. "That Tilexon is a real piece of work."

"Oh dear. What happened, now? I looked at that awful video and when I turned around you had disappeared."

I took a deep breath and started to feel a bit giddy from the earlier adrenaline rush, and the joy of escape. Then I immediately felt guilty because I was enjoying the sweet smell of freedom while Darick was still sharing breathing space with a revolting goblin and a furious wizard.

"It's complicated," I said.

She sighed, and I sensed her frustration. It was always complicated. "I hope you haven't made it worse," she said.

"Er ..." I said.

"What did you do?"

"I'll fill you in later, I promise. Can you do something for me?"

"I can try."

There still seemed to be a strange energy in the city. Pedestrians' faces pinched with worry, and cars being driven more aggressively than usual.

"Tilexon's going to try to transfer Darick to a maximum security prison."

"He can't do that. Noble hasn't even stood trial yet."

"That's what I said."

"But he has the Council's ear," Morgan said. "So ... who knows what he can arrange?"

I nearly rode into a pothole. I swerved just in time and almost T-boned a minibus taxi. I braked hard and nearly lost control of the bike.

"*Deodamnatus,*" I swore.

The driver flipped me the bird and I put out my hand in apology, then started moving again.

"Where would they transfer him to?"

"I don't know."

"Can you find out?"

"I'll try my best."

"Can you stop it?"

"If the Council okays the transfer, no way. I won't have a say. Moose is the boss now, whether they've made it official or not. They're just waiting for an excuse to prise this badge off my office door."

"*Faex*. I'm really sorry about that."

I pictured her shrugging on the other side of the line. "I'll keep you updated on what happens this side. You do the same. It's dangerous out there."

Those last four words pretty much summed up my life. I nodded. "I will."

She was about to end the call.

"Morgan," I said. "What was in that video that everyone was watching?"

"You still haven't heard?" she asked. "Holy smokes, Jax. It's bad. It's ... very bad."

"Tell me!"

"The Hammerskins," she said. "They've declared war."

"What the hex does that mean?"

"They killed the orc Boss."

"No," I said. *Oh no*. Boss was one of the most decent orcs I'd ever met. And because of that, I knew he'd never make it in the cut-throat world of orc politics.

"They filmed it. The beheading."

"The *beheading?*" I exclaimed.

"Filmed it, and posted it on social media. They're sending a message to the rest of the Realm. And if that wasn't enough, they put his head on a spike and put it outside the Khargol residence. You know *Cucina Or'Capone?*"

"I know it," I said.

"It's still there. The head on the spike, I mean. The cops haven't been able to get into the area. The Hammerskins are armed to the hilt. I don't know where they got all the weapons from, but it's like they've been planning this coup for years.

"Or they've had help," I said, thinking of the unholy alliance between the Neo-Nazis and the Silvano Clan. Helping each other claw their way up to snatch at power.

"Either way, it's all falling apart. We dispatched all the officers we could, but I know it won't be enough. Where are you heading?"

I pictured Boss's head on the spike and felt like I had a cold rock in my stomach.

Darick was hiding something from me. He was heading to some maximum security prison. Nilve SaltySnap was missing. Morgan's job was on the line. The Hammerskins and the vampires were seizing power; a violent civil war hovered on the horizon. I felt sick and utterly desperate. There was only one place I could go.

CHAPTER 9
COPPER CLOCKS

W hen I saw Ferra's glowing face, her Scot-red hair plaited into pigtails, and her Viking helmet, I immediately felt better. Entering her steampunk-themed pub, *The Copper Cog & Ale*, was like stepping into another dimension where you could forget your troubles. Vintage lanterns blazed, filling the restaurant with golden light, and the wood fire in the center of the scrubbed flagstone floor radiated a welcoming warmth.

"Jinx!" she shouted, and wiped her hands on her apron. She had been filling snack bowls with salted rosemary chips and the scent followed her as she approached me. She gave me one of her signature bear hugs, squeezing all the air out of me, then pulled away and punched my arm.

"It's been years!" she said, looking me up and down.

"It's only been a couple of days."

"I was talking Dwarf-years," said Ferra, and I heard the

clocks ticking in the background. "It's been too long. I was worried. And you're too skinny."

The hardness in my stomach began to dissolve.

"You always say that."

"And I always mean it! Sit down. I've got something warm for you in the oven."

A pint of *Copper Cog Ale* appeared, as if by magic, at my elbow. I didn't hesitate to have a large gulp of the golden liquid. It was cold and refreshing and perfect and I had to stop myself from drinking the whole thing in one go.

"I love you, Ferra Fernak."

"Och, go on," she said, and disappeared into the kitchen.

"I mean it!" I shouted. And I did.

THERE WERE other magical creatures there, and they seemed to be exchanging worried whispers. Usually the pub was filled with people telling stories and laughing, and cutlery scraping plates, but today the energy was different. Before I had a chance to get too anxious again, Ferra was back with a steaming plate which she expertly slid in front of me. It had the most delicious aroma. The werewolf, who had been sulking inside my stomach, let out a deep, throaty growl.

"Steak and stout pie," Ferra said. "And don't forget to eat your veggies."

The pie's buttery crust was crisp and light, and the unctuous stew glistened in the lantern light. There was also creamed spinach on the plate, finished with parmesan and cracked black pepper. Lemon and thyme potato wedges, and baby carrots and beetroot roasted in maple syrup. It was so delicious and so comforting I almost started to cry.

Ferra stood behind the counter, watching me eat while she chopped apples with a rose-gold knife. Despite being ravenous, I took it slowly and enjoyed every bite.

Then I noticed one of Ferra's children standing behind the counter, staring at me.

"Hello," I said, and smiled. She just looked at me. Sometimes I felt bad for not knowing all of Ferra's kids' names, but in my defense, there were so many of them, and they looked and dressed the same. Ferra got around it by just calling them *skunks*.

"Well, don't just stand there, Skunk," she said to the little dwarf. "Bring your Aunty Jinx some dessert."

The child nodded and pushed her way into the kitchen beyond, and returned carrying a plate larger than her head. Ferra took it from her and ruffled her hair. "Good job. Go get yourself a cookie."

I was sure I wouldn't have space for dessert but when I saw the Pavlova I may have instantly grown an extra stomach. A basket of baked meringue filled with whipped cream and topped with an avalanche of fresh fruit and toasted almonds, drizzled with a strawberry sauce. When I looked up at Ferra I wondered if she could see the cartoon hearts throbbing in my eyes. She took my empty beer glass away and passed me a hot cappuccino I hadn't seen her pouring.

"Thank you, Ferra," I said.

"It's nothing," she said. "It's what mothers do."

That was like a double-edged sword in my heart. On one side, I missed my mother terribly, on the other side, I knew just how fortunate I was to have a surrogate mother in Ferra. It hurt, and it glowed at the same time. I guess that's how life goes.

As I TOOK a sip of my coffee, I heard a voice behind me, and I almost spilled the drink onto my lap.

"I'm looking for Ms. Knight," said the woman. "Ms. Jacquelyn Denna Knight."

I put the cup down and turned on my barstool to look at her. She had long dark hair, olive skin, and she looked around ten months pregnant. I would have described her as willowy if it weren't for her huge, round belly. I didn't sense any magic coming off her, so I assumed she was untouched. She didn't seem to be a threat.

"That's me," I said.

"Oh!" Her hand flew up to her hair—a self-conscious gesture —and she smiled in relief. "I'm so glad I found you."

I couldn't help looking at her stomach. I always felt uncomfortable around heavily pregnant women in public spaces. They were like ticking time bombs, the kind of ticking time bombs I didn't want to be around. To add to the feeling of urgency, Ferra's copper clocks ticked all around us.

"Can I help you?" I asked.

Her eyes were bright hazel-green, and the dark half-moons below them only served to make the iris color pop. She had not been sleeping. I didn't think I would have been able to sleep, either, with that *tick-tick-tick*.

"I'd like to hire you," she said, and pushed an envelope towards me. She looked worriedly at Ferra, who slung her tea towel over her shoulder.

"I'll give the two of you some privacy," said Ferra, as she looked at me. "Don't go without saying goodbye. I have a little something for you."

I nodded, and looked back towards the woman. "Look, I'd love to help you." It wasn't true, strictly speaking. Just being in her presence made me nervous; I didn't think I'd be able to handle it for the duration of a case. Besides, I had to help Darick get out of jail; he needed my full attention. And then there was Liz Durison, wielding her leatherette whip.

The woman sensed my reluctance and put her hands together in front of her, as if she were praying. I noticed a pale mark on her wedding ring finger.

"Please!" she said in a hard whisper, placing her palm on her belly. "Please. I have no family. I'm desperate."

I bit my lip and looked at her. I knew what it was like to have no family. And what kind of person would I be if I turned down a distressed woman who looked like she was about to give birth? Perhaps if I worked her case really quickly I'd be able to solve it before her water broke, and then I'd be in the clear.

"Come with me," I said, and I led the woman—Samantha Farzad—to a more comfortable seating arrangement. I couldn't picture her balancing on a barstool at Ferra's copper counter. We took the private dining room with the chandelier made of brass pipes and antique-looking bulbs, and once she had squeezed in behind the polished table, she looked at me with those startling eyes of hers.

"What is it?" I asked. "What can I help you with?"

"I'm being haunted," she said. "By my dead husband."

CHAPTER 10

STUCK BETWEEN THE CROSSHAIRS OF LUCK AND LOSS

"Is she gone?" asked Ferra, when I came back from seeing Samantha Farzad out.

"She's gone," I said.

"Thank the Void!" said Ferra, pretending to wipe sweat from her brow. "She was making the other customers nervous. I thought she was about to give birth right here by the fireplace, and I've just had the flagstones cleaned."

I frowned at her, and she laughed. "Och, I'm just joking, Jinx. You know I'm not afraid of birth."

She locked the giant front door. I wasn't used to seeing her do that. Usually it stood open twenty-six hours a day.

"Oh, it's not that," I said. "I just don't know how I can help her."

"You'll figure something out. You always do."

"On the plus side, I can pay for my lunch," I showed her the envelope stuffed with cash.

"Your money is no good here," said Ferra, like she always did.

"It's not my money," I said, passing it to her. "It's Farzad's money."

"Groceries," said Ferra, pushing the money back towards me, which reminded me of all the loot I had in my coat pockets, including Darick's cell phone and his bank details. He had also told me to buy groceries. I guess it was time to go shopping.

"But before you go," said Ferra, and she reached behind the counter and brought out a small box wrapped in *Copper Cog* gift-wrapping, tied with a gold ribbon. "I have a little something for you."

"You shouldn't have," I said, but we both knew that I didn't mean it.

"I've been working on this for ages," said Ferra, her cheeks pink from the heat of the kitchen. "I can't wait for you to see it."

I pulled the tail of the ribbon and it came away elegantly in my hand, then the paper curled away, unwrapping itself, revealing a slim rectangular box. I stared at it for a moment.

"Well?" said Ferra. "Go on!"

I lifted the lid. Inside, on a cream satin pillow, was a large intricate brass key with a decorative handle that looked like a skull. The handle was monogrammed JDK.

"Oh!" I said. "It's so beautiful. Thank you."

For a second I was back in that video game, and the ticking points above my head went crazy, as if I had just won a goblin gold jackpot.

"What do you always say you are bad at?" asked Ferra.

I didn't have to think for long. The possibilities were endless. "Singing?"

She shook her head.

"Dancing? Cooking? ... Shopping?"

Ferra reframed the question. "Which *magic spells* do you need a little help with?"

"Too many to mention," I said, but I tried, anyway. "Healing things. Distraction Magic. Portal Magic..."

Ferra's eyebrows arched when I said *Portal Magic.*

I looked down at the key, then back up—relatively speaking —at the dwarf. "Really?" I asked.

Her nutmeg eyes gleamed. "It's a Skeleton Portal Key."

Ferra had designed various things for me over the years, things that had changed my life—and saved my life—more times than I could count. My trench coat was bomb- and bullet-proof, my nano was always ready to help me in a pinch. My high-tech magical crossbow had helped me finish off at least half of the vampires notched on my bedpost at home. I could summon my bike from anywhere in the Realm if I used the Summoning Ring she had created for me.

And now I could portal. It was such a boon. A game-changer.

"This is so amazing, Ferra. Thank you!"

Dare I say it? Dare I say it? Things were looking up.

"You're very welcome, Jinx."

I hugged her and felt emotional again, stuck between the crosshairs of luck and loss. And then there was a crashing at the door.

At first I thought of Samantha Farzad, thinking she had collapsed against the door, but I knew immediately I was wrong. She was a slender woman, and not physically strong. The banging at the door was too loud and violent for a woman of her shape or state. Someone tall and strong was bashing down the door. A few of the customers exclaimed in fright, adjusting their spectacles and their magic wands with suddenly trembling fingers. A couple stood up and backed away from the commotion, but I stood my ground, as did Ferra. Beneath the door I saw the sweeping shadows of at least three agitated men, and I was pretty sure they were armed.

Ferra wrenched a giant display axe off the brick wall. It may have been an antique, but it was as sharp as the tooth of time.

"Get back," she ordered. "Get behind me."

"No way," I said, and I reached for my crossbow.

CHAPTER 11
RAGUK MAGRA

With a roar, the door came blasting off its giant brass hinges and flew a meter into the air, crashing in front of us. Three huge Hammerskins strode in, their greasy shaved heads gleaming with potential violence. The leader wore animal skins and clicking beads, and he looked at us and roared again, as if he were a wild animal; an angry lion.

I could smell his breath from where I stood. Saliva gushed into my mouth and threatened to lurch out. I swallowed it and stood my ground, despite the bile-rising stink and menacing look on the orcs' faces. Their skin was marked with black and red: dirt and blood. They shone with sweat the way cheddar does if left too long in the sun.

"You have no business here," said Ferra, her voice completely calm, even as she clutched the glinting axe. "Leave now," she said, "or you'll be sorry."

They laughed, all three of them. Guffawed at what they thought was a little dwarf housewife with her red pigtails and stained apron. She still had a tea towel slung over her shoulder and she smelled of gravy and cinnamon.

They kept advancing, and Ferra and I steadied ourselves, ready to fight.

There was a little squeak at the door. One of Ferra's children had come to see what the fuss was about. He was standing in the doorway, holding his blankie to his cheek, paralyzed by what he saw. The size and girth of the orcs' bodies were terrifying to me, so I couldn't imagine how they looked to a little dwarf toddler.

"Mama?" he said, then plugged his mouth with his thumb. He was within grabbing distance of the Hammerskins, who separated us. This filled me with a bowel-dissolving fear. I imagined one of the disgusting, snuffling orcs snatching the boy up and squeezing the life out of him. The mental image made my fingers spark with magic. As the waves of fear crashed through me, so did the energy from the Void, and I felt my power build and build until I could feel the sparks everywhere, just under my skin.

The pub fell silent, wondering who would make the next move. Wizards and goblins moved stealthily behind us, shoring us up. The Khargol orcs joined them, clenching and unclenching their fists.

Ferra seemed miraculously unflustered. "Ferdi," she said to the child. *"Khaan roev fir Papa."*

The child blinked twice, then toddled out to call Fighour, Ferra's husband, and I exhaled the breath I had been holding.

Why hadn't they hurt the child? Why hadn't they grabbed him and used him for leverage?

I looked at the leader, and saw the yellow evil in his eyes. I began sweating again.

They hadn't swiped the child because they were going to take everything anyway, and kill anyone who stood in the way. They didn't need leverage. They had brute force and ignorance, and a couple of automatic rifles hanging around their necks. They had the driving savagery of a coup behind them, pushing them forward, urging them to embrace their cruelty.

"By the order of Raguk Magra of Hammerskin Tribe," said the leader, "We're claiming this property."

"You're what?" said Ferra. "I don't think so."

Ferra had saved up for a decade, working in the drudgery of the Copperfield Institute's always-steaming canteen kitchen, to afford to build this place, and it was a phenomenal success from the get-go. She poured blood, sweat, and tears into *The Copper Cog & Ale.* She loved it like she loved her firstborn child—whose name I forget—and would defend it with the same intensity.

Warm, welcoming, and infinitely accommodating, everyone knew that it was the best pub for magical creatures in the entire Realm.

"Central to the city," said the orc. "Big kitchen here and lots of beds in house."

"Perfect," said the orc to his right. "For army."

"No," said Ferra.

I bristled at the brazenness of them, the entitlement. Anger and magic pricked me all over, as if invisible mischievous fae were prodding me with a golden fork.

Suddenly there was a chinking sound behind the counter, and I looked to see what it could be. Fig strode in, fully armored in steel plates and spikes, as if he were planning to fight a dragon in one of Blimaex Abarim's fairytale books for young wizards. He held in his chainmail-gloved hand a medieval flail: a handle with a ball of spikes. He moved in front of us and despite his short stature, the Hammerskins didn't seem to like the look of him, and each took a step backwards.

"What's this?" said the orc who hadn't yet spoken.

Fig spoke through the grate in his steel helmet. "Get out, the lot of you. And don't come back."

They looked at him, uncertain what to do. The dwarf was short, but the spiked ball looked nasty, and perhaps they were thinking of the damage it could do to their meaty ankles. The leader shrugged his gun into a more comfortable position, then pointed the muzzle at Fighour Fernak. His finger twitched on the trigger.

"No!" I shouted, and my own trigger finger jumped, firing the crossbow directly at the orc's chest. A black bolt penetrated him there, and he cried out in anguish. The other two Hammerskins pointed their rifles at me and I tucked and rolled, hoping the wizards and goblins behind me would think to do the same thing. A spray of bullets hailed down on us, and I felt the sting of them hitting me. Ferra's genius trench coat design prevented them from penetrating my skin. A Khargol loyalist behind me was not as lucky, and caught a bullet in the stomach. He howled in pain.

I rolled on the floor, out of the view of the guns, and sprang up when I was around the corner, ready to take aim again. Ferra let out a battle-cry and went after the shorter Hammerskin with her decorative axe. She managed to lodge it in his thigh. It spurted oily orc blood all over the flagstones to the soundtrack of his screams. He gritted his teeth and went after Ferra, who was now unarmed. I swung out from behind the corner, aimed my crossbow at him, and fired. Despite my trembling fingers and less-than-perfect aim, the high-tech heat-seeking arrow found his bulging heart and stopped it from beating, as it had for his leader. It took him a while to die. He lay, jerking and bleeding on the floor, and muttering about his fiancée.

Good riddance, I thought. *I had done her a favor. The fiancée could thank me later.*

Fighour swung his flail at the remaining orc, and it crashed into his knee, buckling it sideways and felling the man. Ferra was up next; she had retrieved her antique axe from the thigh of the leader.

I beat her to it. I had so much magic swirling inside my body that I knew I had to discharge it or face the consequences. I clipped my crossbow to my back and took out my wand. I gathered the pain and panic I felt in my chest and concentrated it into a fiery blue line.

"Fiat Fulgar!" I shouted, and an intense indigo current zinged out of my wand and struck the last Hammerskin in the stomach. He bellowed as he fell, and tried to protect himself from further attack. I stood above him, ready to strike. I was so sick and tired of these bloody Neo-Nazis thinking they could do as they pleased, snatching whatever they liked and terrorizing good people.

One more lightning strike should do it, I thought, and raised my wand again.

"Stop," said a voice. I blinked and looked around. Ferra let the axe drop to the stone floor.

Stop?

"He's unarmed. Leave him be," said Ferra. "Let him tell go back and tell the Tribe they are not welcome here."

"But Ferra," I said. "They'll come back. They'll come back in droves, and they'll take everything."

The copper clocks on the wall kept ticking.

Ferra sighed and rubbed her face. "They'll come back anyway," she said.

CHAPTER 12
ANIMATED WALLPAPER

When I got home I felt shaken to the bone. I couldn't believe that the warmongering Hammerskins were threatening Ferra's family, her business, and her house. *The Copper Cog* was my happy place—my *safe* place—and now it was under attack. If anything ever happened to Ferra I just wouldn't cope. Anger and hopelessness assaulted me, pulled me down inside myself, made me want to disappear. My hands were trembling when I emptied my pockets out onto the spindly kitchen table. Phone; Darick's bag; Hux Kruq's bag; Skeleton Portal Key; the witness testimony stolen from Morgan's office.

I was so restless I couldn't sit down, couldn't focus. I kept thinking of those three ogres smashing down the door of the steampunk pub and letting us know that they were going to take what they wanted. What haunted me most was the picture of the little dwarf toddler holding his blanket to his cheek and how easily the orcs could have killed him. How easily they would kill him.

I couldn't bear to stand in my kitchen. Apart from the fridge which mocked me with its frosty emptiness, there was the ravenous plant. It had completely covered the window, shutting out any sunshine, and had colonized two and a half walls. Its hungry branches and greedy tendrils had opened cupboard doors, cracked wall tiles and smashed plates to the floor. It was like animated wallpaper that just kept growing and penetrating; a horror film in the making. I didn't have the energy to cut back the plant again or clean up the shards of porcelain. My kitchen could remain looking like the aftermath of a Greek jungle party. I made a mental note to keep my boots on.

Avoiding the kitchen, and too on edge to sit down, I walked to my bedroom, passing through a pocket of cold air as I did so. The hairs on the back of my neck stood up.

I shivered. "Hello, Ghost," I said.

Without Darick in it, my bed was only slightly less depressing than my empty refrigerator. I realized I couldn't stay there alone, or I would drive myself mad. But I didn't want to leave, either. I didn't want to face the savage Hammerskins who were terrorizing the city streets. I picked up my pillow and held it to my face, feeling the cool cotton on my skin, and I screamed as loudly as I could. I shouted and swore until my throat was as tired as the rest of my body, then I fell face-forward onto the bed and rolled over, staring at the damp-stained ceiling. Usually I'd pretend the marks were clouds, and I'd try to see shapes in them, but I saw nothing.

My only source of comfort was the fresh-smelling pajamas that Ghost had folded neatly for me and left on the foot of the bed. I brought them up to my face and inhaled the scent deeply, and it reminded me of that moment so long ago when Mom had been cutting bread for lunch and Dad came in, arms full of sun-dried laundry, and he had lobbed a sock at me. I had tried to catch it, but it dropped to the floor. I had looked up at him, and we both giggled.

When had that been? Days before they were murdered? Weeks?

My body ached with the memory, ached with the deep, dark anxiety I had growing in my chest. I closed my eyes, exhausted by it all, and felt my consciousness begin to drift.

My phone started to ring. I hauled myself up off the bed and hurried to where it lay, vibrating, on the kitchen table. Blimaex.

"Hello Mister Abarim," I said. I wasn't sure if I had slept at all, but I was definitely awake, then.

"Ms. Knight," he said. "I'm terribly glad I was able to reach you. Regarding the Darick Noble case, there is a matter of utmost importance we need to discuss."

My breath caught in my throat, and I slowly lowered myself into one of the flimsy chairs, holding onto the tabletop for extra support. It was a precarious position. My kitchen table chairs were so rickety they'd flatter a matchstick.

"I'm afraid I have some bad news," the wizard said.

My knuckles turned white. "I'm listening."

CHAPTER 13
THE EMBER ISLES

I sat at my kitchen table, staring at the Scorpion-branded bag marked DARICK NOBLE, while Blimaex Abarim told me what he knew.

"I don't want you to worry unnecessarily," said the lawyer. "But the news is rather alarming."

"What is it?" I asked, heart hammering against my ribcage.

"My contact at the Scorpions said he had just processed the transfer of Mister Noble from the holding cells in SubT to ... the Ember Isles."

"No!" I yelled, then covered the receiver of the phone while I swore in every shade I could think of.

No no no.

I felt like vomiting.

"Now," said Blimaex. "I don't need to tell you how dangerous the Black Tower on Ember Island is."

"No," I said.

Dangerous was putting it mildly. "*Lethal*" would be a more accurate description. Once you entered, over the giant steel drawbridge that creaked with menace, you didn't come back. Or, at least, you didn't come back as the same person.

"Now, I'll hasten to add that this transfer is highly irregular," said Abarim. "Mister Noble has yet to stand trial, and as I said before, the case against him is paper-thin."

"Then how can they do that?" I asked. "How was the transfer rubber-stamped?"

"The signature was ... Tilexon Musubarin's. He said the suspect tried to escape. There is evidence of damaged cell bars in that dungeon they call a holding jail."

"*Filius Canis!*"

Blimaex cleared his throat. "He also claims that Mister Noble became violent, and is therefore a threat to the officers at the HQ. Hence the speedy move to maximum security. Now, I'd never heard of this Musubarin chap until this case. You said he's a wizard?"

A dirty wizard, I thought. *A total bastard wizard. A crooked wizard who gives ordinary wizards a bad name.*

I swallowed further curse words that crowded my brain and instead tried to focus on a solution.

"He was appointed by the Council," I said. "Do you still have their ear?"

Abarim hesitated. "I wouldn't be able to approach them about this," he said. "I may no longer be on the board but there is still a very specific protocol which must to be adhered to."

"Of course," I said, tapping my foot, thinking.

"And my position as Mister Noble's attorney," he said. "It wouldn't sit right."

"What can we do?" I asked. My stomach was a churning mess. "Darick can't go to the Tower. No way. I'm not going to let it happen. I'll hijack that Ember Isles transfer van if I have to."

My spiking anxiety made me suddenly excessively thirsty, so I braved the kitchen jungle to pour myself a glass of water. Turning on the tap made the pipes groan. It sounded like my building's insides were as troubled as mine.

"I don't think you'll have to go to such extremes," said Blimaex. "Once I heard about the transfer, which was supposed to happen this evening, I immediately lodged an appeal."

"An appeal? Do you think that will work?"

"Even if it doesn't, it will buy us another twelve to twenty-four hours by delaying the collection."

"Thank you," I said. "Thank you, Mister Abarim."

At least Darick would be safe that night. It was something.

I remembered then that I needed to pay Abarim for his legal counsel. I opened Darick's clear bag and took out his mobile phone. I scrolled for his bank details, then logged into his online banking with his Paragon app. The numbers were reversed, he had said, so I typed in the account number, the branch code, and the roving password backwards, and I was allowed access. It all went more smoothly than I had expected, but when I saw Darick's bank balance, I almost spat out my water.

Holy, holy faex, I thought. *I was not expecting that.*

There were seven digits in his bottom line. And this was just his checking account.

So, not only was Darick Noble crazy good-looking, and tender, and kind—when he wasn't assassinating people—he was also extremely wealthy. I felt like the air had been knocked out of my chest—in a good way.

"You still there, Jacquelyn?" asked Blimaex, who I had temporarily forgotten about.

"Yes!" I said. I may have been panting slightly as I stared at the eye-watering bank balance. "Yes. Still here."

I quickly made a rather generous payment into Abarim's account. Darick's phone made a tweeting sound as I forwarded the proof of payment, as if I had paid the wizard by pigeon carrier instead of a magical banking app.

I meant to click off the screen and lock the phone, but something in the list of transactions caught my eye. There were loads of payments for the same—large—amount, and all from the same company, which showed up as an unintelligible code. Of course, I hadn't meant to snoop. It just comes naturally to me, given my day job. I especially didn't mean to scroll down to see if there were any other interesting things to see. That's when I recognized the account number of Uragh, my odiferous orc landlord, and saw the payment that roughly equalled six months of my rent. The beneficiary description read: RENT - JD KNIGHT.

"LODGING AN APPEAL IS ONE THING," said the wizard. "We need to prove reasonable doubt if we want the case against Mister Noble dropped in its entirety. I'm sorry to say this, but I don't trust that this Moose chap will do the right thing."

"What do you mean?"

"The transfer was his idea. Once he hears of the appeal, I'm sure he'll have another trick up his sleeve to get Noble sent away. He doesn't strike me as the kind of wizard who gives up easily."

"But how can we prove anything without a trial?" I asked. The trial date hadn't even been set yet. If Tilexon had his way, Darick would be languishing in a dungeon at the bottom of the Black Tower before the judge even read the arraignment sheet.

"Our success in beating these charges will hinge on one thing," said Blimaex.

"What?" I asked. I was ready to do whatever it took to get Darick away from Tilexon's extended claws.

"Do you remember what I told you, that the lynchpin of the prosecutor's case is the testimony of the head nurse at Silver Wing?"

"Yes," I said.

"It's all they have. The circumstantial evidence of that singular testimony."

"Kim Smith," I said. "The super reliable witness."

"Bingo," he said.

"I need to get rid of her," I murmured.

I didn't mean in the Orc Mafia way. I didn't mean I needed to poison her with *Indigo Violent* in her sleep. I could plan something much more pleasant. A family vacation to the Khargol Isles, perhaps, or a luxury cruise around the world. A Buddhist retreat in Ixopo where she could take a vow of silence for a couple of weeks, just until the trial was concluded. Kim Smith was a hardworking nurse. She deserved it.

"Heavens," said Blimaex. "Do be careful what you say."

"I didn't mean get *rid of her*," I said. "I meant send her on a nice holiday somewhere tropical...a peaceful place without a phone signal."

I heard something happening on Blimaex's side; a shuffling of paper, perhaps. Then he intoned away from the receiver, "*Thank you, Willard.*"

He returned to our conversation with a sigh. "*I* knew what

you meant, but imagine for a second that a certain detective was listening in?"

Abarim was right. I was usually paranoid enough not to make mistakes like that, but the idea of Darick in a cold mucky dungeon in the Black Tower was really unsettling. I needed to up my game. Focus. Think of a brilliant plan.

"I need to think of a brilliant plan," I said.

"Well," said Blimaex. "Best make it snappy. Along with a rather generous whisky on the rocks, my butler just brought me a note from that contact of mine at the Scorpions."

I swallowed hard.

"Apparently," Abarim said, "Detective Musubarin heard about the appeal and somehow wrangled Judge Valar into attending an 'emergency interview' with the witness, Kim Smith. If the judge believes her story, there's no telling what they'll do."

"Where is this meeting? When?"

"Scorpion headquarters, this afternoon. Four p.m."

"Four p.m.?" I yelled. The clock on my phone read three forty-six.

"Musubarin is trying to convince the judge that Noble is a cold-blooded killer. He is, no doubt, trying to dismiss the appeal and push Noble's transfer through."

I cursed again, under my breath. Three forty-seven. There was no way I could get there in time, and even if I did, I wouldn't be able to stop the meeting. And if I tried to see or speak to Kim Smith, I'd get arrested quicker than you could say *tropical cruise* (or *Indigo Violent)*.

Three forty-eight.

"Jax," said Blimaex, using my nickname for the first time. "If there is anything you can do to stop this meeting, do it."

CHAPTER 14
PET SPECTER

I ended the call and paced the balding carpet of my apartment, my head rioting with panic and possible solutions, and interrupted periodically by my wonder at Darick's wealth, the more-than-generous freelancing payments, and the fact that he had pre-paid my rent for me. I pushed those thoughts from my mind and forced myself to concentrate on the problem at hand, even though it felt impossible to change the outcome of that four p.m. meeting.

Three forty-nine.

In eleven minutes or so, Judge Valar would be sitting down with Musubarin and Sister Smith, and going over her witness statement. I stopped pacing and stared at the sheet of stolen paper on the table.

What if..., I thought. *What if I could somehow change the statement? Not just on the piece of paper, but in real time as she spoke to the judge?*

As if Ghost had heard my thoughts, a cold breeze picked up —despite all the windows being closed—and the page filled with Kim Smith's handwriting trembled and moved just a fraction. I was no ghost whisperer, but I thought that my pet specter may have been urging me on.

"How, though? *How?*" I demanded, even though there was no living person to answer me. I slumped down on the horrid charity-shop chair and rubbed my temples as I wracked my brain. *There must be a way,* I thought. *There must be a way.*

Pictures of Darick being tortured in the depths of the Black Tower haunted me. I heard his screams, like I had that night in the volcano pocket realm when he was being attacked by vampires, and I couldn't bear it. I couldn't let that happen. No matter what, I wouldn't let that happen. I squeezed my temples tighter, as if putting pressure on my skull would light up my brain, but all it did was make my head ache.

Three fifty-two.

They were probably all meeting at the reception desk now, greeting each other politely. Moose was probably thanking Smith effusively for coming in despite her grueling work schedule.

A thankless job, I imagined him saying, *but we really appreciate your service to the country and to the Realm.* I pictured Kim Smith responding with a tight smile, just wanting to get the bloody thing over with.

They've already asked me the same questions ninety-nine times, she would be thinking. She was having nightmares about the incident as it was, without having to repeat the same story over and over.

Despite not knowing Kim Smith from a bar of soap, I felt a sudden and surprising empathy for her. I imagined her in her sensible tan rubber-soled loafers—or perhaps running shoes, for additional arch support—and I could almost feel the deep ache in her muscles from pulling her third double-shift that week. Could feel how she was just desperate to get home and have a hot cup of tea and an episode of *Eastenders* before falling into a troubled sleep on a mattress that needed replacing.

Three fifty-five.

This feeling of slipping into the head nurse's shoes gave me the brilliant idea I was looking for—if brilliant ideas were known to get you into deep, deep trouble. I looked up at the grubby ceiling and thanked the Void for making me just a little bit crazy, because only people who were slightly off their rockers would attempt what I was about to. It wasn't going to be pretty, and the consequences were potentially dire, but Darick had endangered his life to save mine on multiple occasions, and now it was my turn to save his.

CHAPTER 15

SWEET AS A POISONED PEACH

I grabbed the sheet covered with Kim Smith's neat, hard-edged handwriting and held it to my chest. With my fingertips I could feel the impression of the words on the back of the paper, a reversed braille. Next, I went over to my bookshelf, where there was a certain black magic potion burning its way through the dusty shelf. *Spiritus Morbus,* said the fading label. Voodoo Serum. It's what I nicked from Slyden Abarim's sorcery chamber after I had temporarily crippled him with a lightning bolt to his nether regions. If you're feeling sorry for the old bugger, don't. He was as evil as Freddy Krueger, but had only half the charm. I looked at the smoked-glass vial in my hands, summoning the courage to unstopper the bottle. Despite the clock ticking in my head, I closed my eyes for a moment and breathed in deeply.

Yes, I am going to make use of a potion that is banned by the Council.

Yes, using prohibited substances gets you arrested and thrown into magical prisons and labor camps, and...

Yes, I was going to do it anyway.

I pulled the rubber cork out with my teeth and spat it out, then gulped down the contents of the bottle.

The texture was oily and gritty; murky in the worst way. As bitter as apple-seed cyanide, sweet as a poisoned peach. Fruity, but not fresh. Like apricots that lie beneath the tree for too long and are penetrated by worms and flies and turn to bubbling slime inside their sagging skins.

I shuddered and moaned with disgust at the feeling that was traveling inside me. My stomach lurched, but I covered my mouth and swallowed the vomit that threatened to erupt. If there is such a thing as turning green, I think I must have. My insides squelched and simmered, and all I could focus on for two whole minutes was clutching at my stomach and keeping the serum down.

When the sour saliva stopped rushing into my mouth, and my insides stopped roiling, I began the magic spell. I flopped into a chair and looked at the sheet of paper in my hands. I blinked at the uniform handwriting, the way the nurse wrote her name, the way she crossed her Ts. I tried to slow my breathing and think again what it was like to be in Kim Smith's rubber-soled shoes.

Suddenly, my head snapped back against the chair, and I felt my eyes rolling back. My lips were cold and numb.

Spiritus Morbus. Voodoo Serum. Contagious Magic.

If you own something intimate of someone's: DNA, underwear, or a handwritten note, you can use the potion to sling your magic over to them no matter where they are in the world. Slyden Abarim had used it to carve a fairytale into his brother's skin, almost killing him in the process. Right now, the magic was funneling my mind into Kim Smith's body. I would borrow her for only as long as necessary to set the record straight. That was my plan, anyway.

I FELT myself drifting over to the Scorpion headquarters, as if I had died and my spirit was flying over to Musubarin to haunt him till the end of his days. My soul stopped just short of the slow-sweating detective, and I slipped, neatly and quietly, into Kim Smith, who was sitting at the table opposite him. Once I arrived, I blinked, trying to orientate myself and get used to the odd sensation of camping out in someone else's body. The sounds and voices in the room seemed amplified at first; there was an echo, and bright lights, but then I got used it, and I coughed to clear my throat and straightened my spine. Or, rather, I straightened Kim Smith's spine.

"You've turned pale all of a sudden," said Musubarin. "Are you all right?"

He was talking to me. I coughed again and nodded. "I'd just like some water, please."

The detective gestured at the officer at the door to fetch some.

"Judge Valar will be here shortly," said Musubarin. "She's just arrived downstairs."

I turned my head to look at the old bashed-up black-framed clock on the wall. It was three fifty-nine.

The eager officer returned with a plastic bottle of water and handed it to the detective, who took it without saying thank you.

"Thank you," I said to the cop, and he nodded, and the clock struck four.

CHAPTER 16

BLACK BLOOM OF GUILT

A handsome elven woman appeared at the door. Despite her maturity—I put her at around sixty— her face glowed with youth the way elves' skin invariably does, much to most dwarfs' discontent. Judge Valar was tall and had straight blonde hair with subtle silver highlights. She wore a beautifully cut cream robe, and held an expensive briefcase in both hands.

Musubarin shot up out of his chair when he saw her, and offered her a chair, scraping the metal legs on the floor as he did so. The noise reverberated through my ultra-sensitive borrowed body and I had to shift my jaw to release the tension in it.

It felt seriously odd to sit there, just across from a man who hated me so, in a body that felt so peculiar. I was so used to being tall, and strong. Kim Smith's muscles ached like mine did, but in different places, in a different way. Her lower back was sore, her neck and shoulders had very little mobility. Her feet were hot and swollen from her double shift at the hospital. The strangest thing by far was that the real Kim Smith had not disappeared. She was still there; I could feel her. If I concentrated hard enough, I could sense her thoughts. I could taste the memory of the chocolate bar she had quickly munched on her way to the HQ. I could feel her stoicism and her usually perky personality. But she was feeling down, her mood unusually depressed. Anxiety slowly tracked up her spine. She had something on her mind, and I wanted to know what it was.

"Your honor," said Musubarin, "thank you for coming through today. I do so appreciate you taking the time off your busy schedule to attend."

He closed the door behind her. The judge sat down, unsmiling, and clasped her hands together on the table in front of her. She looked at the detective. "I'm missing my only grandchild's end-of-year concert to be here," she said. "I do hope you'll make it worth my while."

Musubarin looked pained for a second, then he got on with business. "It should only take ten minutes. Let's start."

I wondered who exactly was pulling the strings, then, to get a judge to interrupt her day for an "emergency" meeting. Who was orchestrating this, and what did they have on Judge Valar? But these tangled thoughts were too complicated for me to unravel, being in someone else's head with their random thoughts, their nerves, and the haze that came with it. Kim Smith had no children, I learned, when she searched her memory for an image of a children's concert and came up blank, save for what she had seen in Hollywood movies. Working the kind of hours she did in the ICU didn't leave much time for dating (or raising offspring). Sometimes it made her sad, sometimes it was a relief. She couldn't imagine caring for patients all day and then coming home and still having to cook dinner. She was happy with her two-minute noodles and her Pick-n-Pay supermarket pre-made meals. She could make a family lasagne last for five days, and a chicken pie fed her for three. She tried to avoid the junk food dispenser at the hospital, but sometimes it had an almost paranormal control over her, and she'd find herself stuffing coins into its scratched mouth without even truly deciding to. The thought of the snack dispenser pulled at something else in her conscience, a black bloom of guilt like an ink drop falling into water, but she pushed it away. I tried to grab onto it, tried to read it, but it disappeared before I had the chance to have a proper look. I wanted to get it back, but I didn't know how.

"Your honor," said Musubarin, touching his broken and bruised nose for effect. "We have a dangerous criminal down below in SubT. This morning I caught him trying to escape."

Pants on fire! I wanted to yell. I tried to keep my cool, although I couldn't help side-eyeing the deceitful detective.

Musubarin slid Darick's case file towards the judge, and she opened it. Her nails were perfectly painted in a kind of iridescent pearl. Kim Smith looked down, self-consciously, at her own neglected nails, and hid them under the table.

"There was significant damage done to the steel bars," he said. "I worry that our security here is not strong enough to restrain him. If he manages to escape, there's no telling how many people he will harm."

Valar paged through the first section of the file, and I saw the mugshot of Darick that I first noticed in Blimaex Abarim's magical notebook.

"Now, the accused's attorney lodged an appeal to delay the transfer of Mister Noble to a more secure location. I'd like that appeal denied so that I can ensure no one else is hurt."

Valar paged to the end, then frowned at the information before her and tapped at it with a long, slender finger.

"Where's the rest of the file?" she asked. "Where's the evidence of the crime he is accused of?"

Ha! I thought. Maybe Valar wasn't on anyone's payroll, after all.

Moose shifted in his chair and leaned forward. "Your honor, I'm sure that after interviewing Sister Smith here, you'll be as convinced as I am around the accused's guilt."

"But this is not a court of law," she said. "And suspects are innocent until proven guilty. Is that not so?"

"Yes, but—"

"Detective Musubarin, I hate to state the obvious, but Boulderkeep and the Black Tower are for *convicted* criminals."

"But if you only knew how dangerous he was," he said, and pressed his fist to the table. "Don't you see that if you leave him here, more people could die?"

Valar didn't flinch; she just gave him an acidic glare. His nostrils were flaring as he tried to remain calm. He wiped the sheen from his forehead and tried again, in a softer voice.

"He tried to strangle a little old lady," the detective said. "While she was unconscious and recovering from a brutal attack—"

I had to admit, he knew how to use words for maximum effect. Employing *brutal attack,* as if Darick had done it. *More people could die. Strangling. Little old lady.* Perhaps he should have been a lawyer instead of a hack detective.

"Your honor. I'm not asking you to convict him. I'm just asking you to deny the appeal. We cannot delay the transfer of Darick Noble. If he stays here, and if he escapes, as I know he will," said Tilexon, glaring right back at Valar, "and he kills anyone, then those innocent peoples' blood will be on our hands."

It was clear that Musubarin meant that the blood would be on the judge's hands.

"All right," she said, putting her elbow on the table and pinching the bridge of her nose. "I agree that if Noble is as dangerous as you say, he needs to be in a maximum security establishment. I'll arrange for the trial date to be moved forward, and I'm willing to deny the appeal blocking the transfer if I find the witness's statement conclusive."

Musubarin's relief was palpable. Valar pursed her lips and turned her attention to me. "Sister Smith," she said. "Please, tell me what you saw."

CHAPTER 17
A CLOUD IN A JAR

I took a deep breath and hesitated to speak. I didn't know where to start. I couldn't blurt out whatever story I wanted to. It had to be convincing. Musubarin saw me stalling and tried to help things along. He looked at me in what he probably thought was a kind and understanding way and steepled his hands on the desk.

"Sister," he said. "Can you tell us exactly what you saw when you approached Hettie Frost's private ward yesterday morning?

Was it only yesterday? I felt like I had aged a hundred years since I heard that Darick was arrested.

"Er—" I said. My foreign body felt awkward, my voice alien. "Well."

Judge Valar looked at me expectantly. I imagined that she was trying her best not to drum her fingertips on the government-issued gray metal table we were sitting around, the surface of which was cool on my perspiring palms.

"I was doing my rounds," I said, "when I heard the alert on the heart monitor in Frost's ward start beeping." Kim Smith's accent came easily to me, as if I had been born with it. Which, in a way, I guess I had been. "When I got to the door, I saw that the police officer on duty was asleep outside. The door was open just a crack. I felt the officer's pulse, in his neck, and it was very weak. He wasn't just sleeping. Someone had knocked him out. I got a fright, then."

"Why?" asked the judge.

"Hettie Frost's room was under police protection. The reason she was in ICU was because she had been attacked the day before, and as far as the nursing team knew, the attacker was still on the loose. The police were worried he may come back and—"

"Finish the job?"

"Yes," I said. "So when I entered the room, I was already thinking the worst. Thinking that whoever was in there was trying to harm my patient."

"You're saying that you had already made up your mind before you entered the room?" asked Valar. "You thought you'd be finding the killer standing there?"

"I'd already had nightmares about the killer the night before," I said, my voice wobbling just a little. "I couldn't imagine someone hurting an old lady like that. And to think, in the end, it was actually a woman! The nursing team and I weren't expecting that."

"Hold on," said the judge. "Slow down. You've lost me. Which woman?"

"It's not important," said Musubarin. "Sister, let's not get stuck in the weeds. What did you see when you walked into—"

"I'm actually interested in the weeds," said the judge, giving Moose a withering look. "I happen to be fond of weeds."

Musubarin set his jaw again and looked at the relentless clock on the wall.

"Tell me," said Valar. "Which woman?"

"Well, the killer," I said. "The witch hunter. The attacker who buried Hettie Frost alive. Ophelia Knox killed three women from the StarDust Coven before she was arrested."

"That is yet to be proven," said Musubarin, shifting in his seat.

"It can take time," I said, looking straight into the detective's eyes. "But I believe that justice will be served."

"Okay," said the judge. "So, as far as we know, Darick Noble had nothing to do with the StarDust Coven murders."

"Right," I said.

Musubarin was looking at me, puzzled, wondering why I had changed my tune, but still hoping I'd deliver the testimony they needed.

"But you didn't know that at the time," said the judge. "You imagined the killer to be male, and when you entered Frost's ward you saw an unknown man standing at her bed."

"Yes," I said. "The more I think about it, the more I wonder how much my initial panic colored my experience."

Musubarin couldn't sit still. "What was Noble doing when you walked in?" he asked.

"He had his hands on Hettie," I said.

"He was strangling her," said Tilexon.

"I'm not sure if he was *strangling* her," I said.

"Detective," snapped Valar. "If you lead this witness one more time, this interview is over."

"It's in her witness statement!" yelled Moose. "In black and white. She walked in on him strangling the old lady!"

"Detective," warned the judge. "I'm warning you."

Musubarin grabbed the case file from in front of Valar and tore it open, looking desperately for the handwritten testimony, which I happened to be holding in my original body sixteen kilometers away from where I was sitting right now.

Musubarin slammed the file shut again and wrenched open the door.

"Morgan!" he shouted. "Morgan!"

"I'm not sure he was *strangling* her," I said, pretending to think. "He could have been. Or it could have been a ... massage?"

"A *massage?*" cried Musubarin, his eyeballs threatening to spontaneously pop out of his head.

"I thought perhaps he was the new physiotherapist. We were expecting a new physio on the block."

"A new *physiotherapist?*" There were flecks of saliva flying out of his mouth. "And that's why you screamed bloody murder? I mean, you literally screamed."

Oh. I had forgotten that Smith had screamed.

"As I said before, I got a terrible fright."

"Why is there no mention of massages or physiotherapists in your sworn statement?" demanded Moose.

"Calm down, Detective," said Valar. "You're coming close to bullying the witness. And as far as I can tell, she's your only one. So if I were you, I'd simmer down."

"I think I was in shock," I said. "The more I think about that moment, the more I realize that I overreacted. It's not an easy thing to admit to," I said, attempting a wry smile but perhaps not quite pulling it off. "I'm known for my nerves of steel at the hospital."

Captain Morgan strode past the window without glancing in on us and stopped, putting her hand on the doorway. For a moment I forgot who I was, and I smiled at her. She narrowed her eyes and shot me a suspicious look.

"What is it, Moose?" she asked. "I've got things to do."

"Get me that witness statement on the Noble case," he said.

"Did your mother not teach you manners?" someone asked. Then I realized the question had come from me.

Everyone in the room kept quiet and looked at me, and a hot blush crept up my neck and burst onto my cheeks.

"She's right, you know," said Valar. "Your manners could do with a little work."

Musubarin was ready to launch into an apoplectic fit. Instead, in a deadly voice, he told Morgan to get the statement.

"It's not in my office," she said. "As soon as I realized it was missing, I searched for it. It's gone."

"It's your job to look after the dockets in your care," said Moose.

"It's okay," I said. "I'll write a new one."

"Thank you," said Morgan.

"The more I think about it," I said. "The more I think that I totally overreacted. I'm sorry I wasted your time."

Musubarin shoved his hand in my direction, and then narrowed his eyes at Morgan. "You did this."

She looked genuinely shocked. "Me?"

"You're friends with that troublemaker. Jacquelyn Denna Knight."

The mention of my name made me blush again, and it did something else, too. It seemed to weaken the contagious magic, as if it were reminding me of who I really was. I felt like my spirit was detaching itself from Smith's body. I was being torn down a perforated line.

Morgan frowned, crossed her arms and angled her head at him. It was a good look, with her red lipstick and slightly masculine, stylish clothes. "You're obsessed with her," said Morgan. "My advice is to get out more."

Musubarin slammed his hand down on the table, making me jump and further detach from Kim Smith's body. I tried to hold on. I needed to stay until the meeting was over or there'd be a lot of explaining to do.

"I've heard enough," said Judge Valar. "This case was shaky to begin with, Tilexon, but now it's on the Richter scale. You've got nothing."

I was so relieved that I slumped back in the hard plastic chair, and my feet danced a little jig under the table, swollen ankles and all.

"In fact," Valar said. "You don't even have enough to hold him here, never mind send him off to the Ember Isles."

"Don't say it," Musubarin pleaded, but the judge was undeterred. On her way out, she addressed Morgan.

"Captain, unless you have an objection, please arrange for the release of Mister Noble, first thing in the morning, with Detective Musubarin's apologies."

"Yes, your honor," said Morgan.

Musubarin gave me a glare so icy it could have frozen a flame. The judge hurried out, and I thought that perhaps she might be able to catch the final set of her grandchild's concert.

"WHAT THE HELL WAS THAT ABOUT?" he said to me in a hard whisper. I shrugged my stiff shoulders, but I knew I was losing control over my borrowing of Kim Smith's body because her arms just moved in jerky little movements. I was floating away, and I just hoped that there was enough residue left over from my visit that the nurse didn't kick up a fuss. Perhaps she would now consider the idea that she had overreacted when she saw Darick in that ward.

"Don't speak to the witness like that," commanded Morgan. "And I'd appreciate it if you didn't yell out my name like that, like you did before. I'm not your lackey."

I tried to make myself as heavy as possible, leaning down, trying to stay in Smith's body, but it was no use. It was like trying to catch a cloud in a jar.

"You lost a crucial piece of evidence!" yelled Musubarin. "You sabotaged this case, and I'm going to make sure you pay for it."

"You know that's not true."

"You're fired!" he shouted.

Morgan guffawed. "I'm *what?* Have you forgotten that I'm the boss here?"

"Not anymore," said Musubarin, and wiped the froth from

his lips with the back of his hand. "And you'll be in a disciplinary hearing first thing in the morning."

Morgan's face turned as white as the cheap drywall behind her. "Excuse me?"

I really wanted to stay in the room to listen to the argument, but they were fading away.

"You know that management meeting I was in this morning?" asked Moose. "You're being demoted."

"Bull," Morgan said, but her face remained pale.

He reached into his pocket with a sneer and brought out a bright new name badge: CAPTAIN MUSUBARIN, it said, and the tail of the red scorpion on the logo had never looked so vicious.

CHAPTER 18
A DUMPSTER FIRE OF MAGNIFICENT PROPORTIONS

When I snapped back into my body, my neck was stiff, *al a* Kim Smith, and my mouth was dry. It took me a few minutes to figure out where I was. Two sets of animal eyes were staring at me: Kresnik's pair of shiny black beads, and the small pink marbles of Gizmo.

A raven shifter and a magical albino ferret walked into a bar, I thought. But then I couldn't think of a funny punchline, so I abandoned the joke and massaged my shoulders, instead. After feeling the effects of the potion immediately after drinking it, I had expected the hangover of all hangovers when I returned to my real body, but it actually wasn't too bad. Nothing like the comedown and the withdrawal symptoms that I'd had from the Vampire Venom a few days before. Once I stood up, I felt quite light, and I shook my body around to get my circulation going again. No headache, no lava in my stomach. The success of my mission dawned on me slowly. My plan had worked, and Darick would be a free man in the morning. I high-fived myself.

Darick would get out of jail and we'd live happily ever after.

The daydream only lasted for a moment before reality came crashing in. There was civil war on the horizon; Ferra and her family were in danger; SaltySnap was still missing; and Morgan was on the cusp of losing her job. Musubarin was clawing his way up the ranks; the Council seemed crazy; and, judging by the self-styled *Little Shop of Horrors* plant taking over my kitchen, I guessed that the vampires were building their pocket realm more and more each day. Soon their collective power would eclipse all the good magic and the Realm would turn into a dumpster fire of magnificent proportions. I sat down again, almost squashing a surprised Gizmo in the process, and I buried my face in my hands. The ferret forgave me for almost snuffing him, and crawled onto my lap, where I stroked his soft fur.

Kresnik cawed. Bron was still stuck in his raven form, and I didn't know what to do about it. As far as my hexing magic knowledge went, I vaguely remembered that certain hexes could only be overturned by the witch or warlock who cast the spell, which would be tricky, seeing as Ophelia was probably on her way to Boulderkeep.

"I'll find a way to break the spell, Bron," I said. I just needed a little time. There would be another way, I just needed to find it.

My main objective at that moment was to not feel totally overwhelmed by what was out of my control. Yes, things were falling apart all around me. It was like standing in Hillbrow on New Year's Eve where people inexplicably start throwing their possessions out of their windows. Televisions, radios, old couches. It's not safe to walk around Hillbrow on most days of the year, but hanging out there on New Year's was like playing a unique game of Russian Roulette. I felt like I was going to be crushed by a hurtling home appliance any minute. An old fridge, I thought, with our love-hate relationship, would be fitting.

I DECIDED to focus on the things I *could* control, which, admittedly, were few and far between. What could I do while I waited for Darick to be released? Then Samantha Farzad's dark crescent-mooned eyes came to me. With the attack on *The Copper Cog* earlier, I had completely forgotten that she had asked for my help—and already paid me for it. I agreed to meet her at her haunted house hours ago, and the sun was already setting. Because of the sudden arrival of the dark, I was tempted to stay home and text her that I'd come by the next morning, but then I thought of her so heavily pregnant, scared, and alone in her house. I needed to go to her right away.

CHAPTER 19
ORPHANOS

Instead of taking my trusty motorbike, I thought it would be safer to give my new Skeleton Portal Key a try. I still felt a little lightheaded from the *Spiritus Morbus*. Taking the bike, at night, when I wasn't quite feeling myself probably wasn't a great idea. Also, there were reports of bombing and looting on the city streets coming through on my phone, and the last thing I wanted was to be pulled over by a rage of Hammerskins. Gizmo complained when I took him off my lap; he wanted to go with me.

"I think you guys should stay here," I said to him and Kresnik. "I won't be gone for long." But when I pulled on my trench coat, Gizmo jumped into my arms, scurried up, and disappeared into my infinity pocket.

"All right, then," I said. Who was I to argue with a magical albino ferret?

Then Bron, the raven, snapped his wings, swooped, and

landed on my shoulder. He nodded his charcoal-feathered head at me, his black beak shining in the fading light.

Trust Jacquelyn Denna Knight to have rebellious familiars, I thought.

I picked up the key from the kitchen table and looked at it. Knowing Ferra's engineering capabilities I didn't doubt that it would work perfectly, but attempting Portal Magic of any kind was still a bit nerve-wracking. There were always urban legends being exchanged in whispers at the Copperfield Institute about careless wizards who landed up in dangerous or embarrassing situations by not visualizing their locations vividly enough, or by enunciating poorly. One of the stories was about a wizard who had appeared on a train track at the very wrong second and was met by the front bars of a barreling train. It was in the small snowy Siberian town of Dikson (perhaps his Russian accent left something to be desired) and he ended up frozen solid to the steel pilot of the train.

I tried to shut off the stream of the other macabre schoolyard tales as I focused on the key. With Ferra's genius magical tech, a ferret GPS, and some clear focus, I shouldn't have a problem.

Famous last words, my nerves chimed in, but I ignored them.

I GUESSED that Ghost might not want me to go out. The phantom could get overprotective sometimes, but never overbearing. I thought he might decide to rearrange my reading material for me by slamming a couple of books on the floor, but he did not. Maybe he was in a really good mood, or maybe he had stopped caring about my wellbeing. I hoped it was the former, because as an orphan I needed all the surrogate parents who would have me, generous red-haired dwarfs and vigilant ghosts included.

Sometimes I thought I should stop calling myself an "orphan." Despite my clear lack of talent for adulting, I couldn't deny that I was no longer a child. Does one ever grow out of one's orphan status? I was caught between wanting to move on and leave the trauma of losing my parents behind, and not wanting to ever forget them. I clung to the few memories I had like a baby chimp clings to her mama. I had looked the word up in the dictionary a few years before and it described an orphan as a child whose parents are dead, but the origin of the word is late Latin from Greek *orphanos*, which means "bereaved." I may no longer be a child, but my bereavement has never left me.

I CHECKED my phone for Samatha Farzad's address to make sure I got the location spell completely correct. With Gizmo in my pocket and Kresnik on my shoulder, I held the key in both hands, closed my eyes, and focused on the address, imagining it written in clear bold letters in my mind.

"Ianua Sit," I chanted, and the key began to feel warm in my palms, almost hot. I thought of Farzad's address again in clear block letters. Gizmo squeaked, and Bron ruffled his feathers.

There was a small explosion of golden butterflies in my stomach and it felt like my body was dividing into 3D pixels, little blocks of wizard that were humming with potentiality and the excitement of an imminent trip. And then we were off, whipped into the air and rushing through space.

Now, you're supposed to keep your eyes closed while traveling through a portal, or you risk motion sickness and vertigo, but I love watching the pictures flash by. Lonely spirits floating in limbo; sparkling stars so close you feel like you can reach out and touch them; the dead black of space brushed into color by the arctic lights, and the confounding weather: hot rain and cold lightning. And just as you get used to the rushing in your ears, you slow down and there is absolute silence, and then a deep pressure that threatens to squeeze the very life out of you. It feels like your eyeballs will burst. You think your spleen will explode—let's be honest, it wouldn't be missed—but instead, at the last minute, there is a release. You land on the ground of the location of your choice, and hope against hope that there's not a Russian ice-train coming your way.

The landing on my first ever portal spell was pretty rough, and I banged my left knee so hard on the tarmac that I wanted to howl like a dire-wolf. But when I looked up, I was so happy to see the correct house in front of me that the pain immediately receded. Suddenly there was a cloudburst above us, and rain pelted me as I stood up. A lightning bolt lit up the sky behind the haunted house, throwing it into silhouette, and I rushed up the pathway and rang the bell. Gizmo was snuggled safely in my coat pocket, and Kresnik perched on the balcony guard-rail, a feathered sentinel.

The house was quiet and dark, and I wondered if Samantha had given up waiting for me and gone somewhere else. Then I heard her delicate footsteps, and a heavy clunking as the door was unlocked. She looked at me, first relieved, and then concerned, and pulled me out of the driving rain and inside the house, where I dripped on the carpet. There was another streak of lightning, and another rumble of thunder. The house was dark inside. A towel materialized out of nowhere and Sam threw it over my shoulders.

"Thank you," I said.

She smiled tightly and put her hands on her back, which I'm sure was aching, having to carry that huge belly of hers. My nervousness at being around the ticking time bomb resurfaced, and I hoped that her baby wouldn't choose tonight to make an appearance. As if on cue, Farzad grabbed her stomach and winced.

"Oh!" she gasped.

Out of empathy or anxiety, I wasn't sure which, my stomach clenched, too.

"Are you okay?" I asked.

Her expression of discomfort disappeared, and was replaced by a smile. "I was only kidding," she said, and I forgot to laugh.

"It's a good trick," she said. "To get you to the front of a shopping queue. People are practically allergic to full-term pregnancies."

It was an odd moment, standing there in the near dark, dripping, the storm raging outside. I hadn't expected Farzad to have a sense of humor, and it caught me off-guard.

"Come in," she said. "I'll get you a hot glass of tea, and we can go upstairs. My husband is looking forward to meeting you."

CHAPTER 20

HIS CLOTHES WERE MADE OF SMOKE

The peppermint tea looked pretty in the tall, gold-patterned glass, and it was loaded with sugar. The taste reminded me of when we'd use Peppermint Crisp chocolate bars as straws for our lunchtime milk from the canteen at Copperfield. We'd bite off the top and bottom of the chocolate bar and then plunge it into our glasses and use it to siphon up the sweet minty milk. It's a taste I've since grown out of, but the tea brought back the memory in a vivid menthol-flavored flash.

We sat in the lounge upstairs, and settled into an uncomfortable silence. Sam perched on the edge of her chair, her pregnant belly looking bigger than ever.

"Your husband—"

"He'll be here," she said, playing with the silver locket on her necklace, zipping it this way and that, sometimes touching it to her lips. "He visits every night."

I put the tea down on the side table. "Tell me about him."

"Alif," she said. "His name is Alif."

"Tell me about Alif."

"He died a year ago," she said, and waited for that to sink in. When I nodded, she continued. "It's been four seasons, but he hasn't let go."

"He's attached to you," I said.

Sometimes the cords of love are too strong to break, even when the Grim Reaper is around, slinging his scythe.

"I need you to break the bond," she said. "Please."

"You don't love him anymore?"

"It's not that," she said. "It's the opposite."

She loves him too much. She's reminded of her loss every time he visits her.

"You can't move on with your life," I said.

There were tears in her hazel-green eyes. "I can't live like this anymore. It's not healthy. I have to think of the baby."

"You've told him this?"

"I've tried, but I can't seem to get through to him. I'm hoping you'll be able to communicate with him. He was a persistent man when he was alive, and he is even more so now. I beg him to leave me alone, but he still visits every night. I can't sleep. I thought I should move houses, or countries, but I know that won't stop him. Nothing will stop him."

She regarded the window on the opposite side of the room with a blank stare.

"When he was alive, he'd say that as long as we loved each other, we'd be together forever."

"I can't break the bond that tethers him to you," I said. "Only you can do that."

"How?" She asked.

"If you stop loving him, he will let you go."

She buried her face in her hands. "I can't," she said. "I've tried. Don't you think I've tried?"

I didn't want her to get too emotional. Who knows what effect weeping would have on a uterus that was already stretched to breaking point. I changed tack.

"WHAT HAPPENED TO HIM?" I asked. "How did he die?"

There must have been magic swirling around him when it happened; it was the only way a human had any chance of hanging on to the realm of the living.

She shook her head. "I don't know."

I blinked at her. "You don't know how your husband died?"

"It was covered up," she said. "His file was classified. They fed me some fake story but when I started to investigate they told me to stop, or else."

I kept looking at her, trying to figure it out.

"He was a spy?" I asked.

"Yes."

"For the Council," I said.

"Yes."

"And you haven't asked him?"

"We can't ... talk," she said. "We can't communicate in words. That's why I hired you."

THERE WAS A KNOCKING on the window that had earlier held Samantha's attention, and she went to open it. The storm was still boiling the black sky, and rain splattered in on the windowsill. A white razor of lightning slashed the air in front of the house, making us both jump.

Farzad smiled again. "You'd think you'd be used to spooky things," she said, "after being haunted for over a year."

She slammed the window shut again, and I gave her a puzzled look.

"He's here," she said. "He's inside with us now."

She watched me expectantly as I looked around the room, searching for a sign of the ghost. I felt nothing. I started thinking that perhaps Samantha Farzad was crazy—struck mad by grief—and I was filled with dread as I looked at her haunted face and huge belly.

. . .

"I can't feel him," I said. "Are you sure?"

"He's here." The rain bucketed down outside, the thunder rolled, the lightning sliced the black velvet of the sky, filling the room with cold white flashes.

Faex, I thought. *A ghost husband I can deal with. An insane pregnant woman is another box of frogs.*

"Samantha," I said carefully. "Did you go for any counseling after Alif died?"

She flinched as if I had pinched her.

"You think I'm crazy?" she asked. "You think I imagine him coming into my room every night?"

"No," I said. "I—"

She held her stomach. "Do you think I imagined this?"

I rubbed my forehead, trying to get my head around the—rather odd—situation. Alif Farzad had died a year ago, but Samantha was nine months pregnant. The only way that was possible was if—

But then I didn't have to strain my brain, because when I looked at the chair adjacent to mine there he sat, with one leg casually crossed over the other, as if the room belonged to him. Olive-skinned, like Samantha, with dark hair and sparkling jewels for eyes. His clothes were made of smoke. It was clear that he had been watching me all along, sizing me up, deciding whether I could be trusted.

"Oh," I said.

"Do you feel him?" asked Sam.

"I see him," I said. I also saw the sparks of magic flying around him.

Samantha started crying. I looked up at her and asked her what was wrong.

"How does he look?" she asked.

I wasn't sure how to reply.

He looks well, I thought. *For a dead man.*

"You haven't seen him?" I asked Samantha. "Since he passed away?"

"I can only feel him," she said, wiping her eyes. "His body. His thoughts. Sometimes his presence is strong, sometimes it's just a breath on a feather."

I looked directly at the smoking spirit, and I was struck by cold air and goosebumps. I shivered and sat upright.

"Hello," he said. His voice rang out as clear as day, and he seemed rather smug for someone without a beating heart in his body.

The weather raged against the window pane, as if it were a creature trying to get inside.

"Tell him," Sam said. "Please tell him he needs to move on. For the sake of the baby."

I looked at him; watched as the smoke swirled around him, lit by the occasional spark.

"Alif," I said. "What do you need from Samantha to allow you to complete your journey to the other side?"

I hated how I suddenly sounded like one of those fraudulent old fortune tellers who pretended to be able to commune with the dead, but I didn't know how else to phrase it.

Shove off to Halloween Heaven, Dead Guy. Your time is up. Vamanos.

Alif's eyes twinkled at me. "I have a job for you to do, Jacquelyn Denna Knight," he said.

Er, what now?

"How do you know my name?"

He looked amused. "You think it was my wife's idea to hire you?"

I'm pretty sure I looked as thoroughly confused as I felt. I stared at him, then Samantha, who was shivering, then back at him. He started signing an intricate spell with his hands, and the lights got slightly dimmer. A blanket floated off the sofa and arranged itself over Sam's shoulders.

"That's better," he said, and smiled.

The smoke, the magic.

"You're a djinn," I said.

"Sometimes I whisper things into my wife's ears while she sleeps. She can't hear me or see me while she's awake, but somehow when she's dreaming, her mind is more receptive."

"Why did you ask her to hire me?"

"I need you to convince her to die."

CHAPTER 21

THE DEADLING DJINN

"I realize how crazy that sounds," Alif said. "But I hope you'll hear me out."

I stared at the smug djinn; I wanted to hear this. "I'm not going anywhere."

Samantha pulled the blanket tighter around herself.

"When I died," he said. "I didn't go all the way."

"That's pretty obvious," I said. "Given your presence in that chair."

"What I mean is, the magic kept me ... suspended. A safety net, of sorts."

"Which magic? Yours?"

He shook his head. "Djinn magic is not that powerful.

I was dying. At first I fought it, but then a sense of calm came over me. I realized that Death was not the enemy. I decided to relax and let the light take me."

129

I shifted in my seat.

"Then I heard this ... chanting. This magic. It was holding me back."

This made me remember the meeting of the StarDust Coven at the Moonlit Chapel. Hettie Frost had been buried alive by Ophelia and Dylan Knox. She had run out of oxygen and died, but we had brought her back to life. Isadora and I resuscitated her with chest compressions and mouth-to-mouth, while the coven chanted a spell in the background. I still remember the feeling of the cold soil on my skin and the witches' black-ink eyes. Hettie's pale, stiff body and finger-tips scraped to the bone, and how her terrified eyes finally clicked open.

It still bothers me; I always wonder how much of the resuscitation was real and how much was magic. Bringing people back to life using magic is considered a Dark Art, and usually has terrible consequences. Together we had brought Hettie Frost back to life, but Alif had not been so lucky.

"I almost made it," he said. "I was right there, at the soft silver membrane that separates life and death, but it didn't let me through. I couldn't get back to the world of the living, but turning my back on death meant that door was closed to me, too."

"You're a deadling," I said.

I'd never met a deadling before. We had learned about them at the Institute, but it had been a more theoretical lesson than anything else, like learning about alchemic reactions in outer space.

Deadlings are neither alive nor dead. Also known as living ghosts, or breathing spirits, they live between the billowing veils of life and death.

"You must feel trapped," I said.

"It's not like that," he said.

"What's it like?"

"What is he saying?" Samantha asked.

"He said he doesn't feel trapped."

Alif looked at me. "Would you describe being alive as 'trapped'"?

"No," I said. "No."

"Are you sure?" he asked.

"Okay, I guess, sometimes. In a way."

"Well, this is like being alive, but lighter," Alif said. "I don't need to eat or drink. I own nothing. Not even a set of clothes. It's very liberating."

"You make it sound like a nude hippie retreat," I said, and he laughed.

"I definitely don't feel trapped," he said. "I feel the opposite of trapped. I want Samantha to feel it, too."

"You're crazy," I said.

"The Realm is a crazy place."

This was true. But that didn't mean I was going to help him.

Alif started moving his fingers again, casting a spell in sign language. The peppermint tea that had grown cold on the table began to steam, and then his magic lifted it and placed the glass gently in Samantha's hands. She took it gratefully.

"Sam wants you to leave her."

Alif shook his head. "Sam doesn't know what she wants. She's still grieving, and the pregnancy is making her anxious."

"I'm not here to help *you*," I said. "I'm here to help *her*. And she wants you to leave her alone."

"Ms. Knight," the djinn said. "Please take my word that the day that is true, the moment it is true, I will leave her alone. But it is not what she wants."

"Samantha," I said, looking across at her. "Why did you hire me?"

"Because I can't carry on like this," she said. "Not with a baby coming."

"She is suffering," I said. "You have to let her go."

"She is suffering," Alif said. "Let her come to me."

I noticed then that the storm had quieted down.

Reluctantly, I turned to Samantha. "He wants you to join him."

"What?" she said, her eyes flying open. "Do you mean—?"

"You know what I mean," I said. "And I really wouldn't recommend it."

"But we could be together again," he said.

I repeated his words for her. "Then you can be together again."

Turns out I was a pretty good ghost whisperer, after all.

"Is that true? That we could be together again?" Samantha asked.

"I don't know," I said. "I wouldn't even know how to start."

"You'll find a way, wizard."

"I won't," I said.

Sam's face was pale. "What about the baby?"

But no one had an answer for that.

THE DEADLING djinn walked me to the front door, trailing smoke as he floated down the stairs. He had already tucked his exhausted wife into bed and kissed her forehead.

"Please," he said. "We need your help."

"Your wife has not agreed."

What a strange concept to think about. *Your wife has not agreed to die to be with you.*

"She will," he said. "She'll realize it's the only way for us to be together."

I wanted to say: *Well, maybe she wants to* live *more than she wants to be with you,* but I knew it wasn't true. If their relationship status was on Facebook, it would be described as *complicated.*

"Well," I said. "Call me if she ever changes her mind."

I began to leave, but he cascaded in front of me, blocking my way.

"I need your help to change her mind. You need to convince her."

"Um, nope," I said, walking through him. "I'm going home."

His smoke scattered and he formed in front of me again. "It's the only solution," he said.

"Not doing it," I said, and I walked through him again. The grass was wet and muddy, and the black road shone under the yellow streetlight buzzing above us. This time he didn't re-form his spectral self in my path, he just called from behind me.

"I have information for you, Jacquelyn Denna Knight."

I stopped and slowly turned around.

"What kind of information?"

"I get to see things," he said. "Being a deadling has a … unique point of view."

"I don't know what that means."

"Well," he said, his smoke swirling beautifully in the cool night air, "I know how you can find your parents."

I reeled. I felt as if he had punched me in the stomach.

"My parents are dead," I said.

Is that what he meant about the unique viewpoint? Could he see into the Afterlife as he was seeing into the land of the living?

"Tell me what you know," I said.

Alif smiled. "But then what would I use to convince you to help us?"

CHAPTER 22

A GRAY-COLORED DREAM

Feeling angry and self-destructive, I decided to ride my bike home. I touched my summoning ring and my motorbike arrived in a cloud of black glitter.

How dare the deadling djinn try to manipulate me like that?

I smashed my smart helmet over my head. I didn't like the djinn one bit, the way he was so forceful with his wife, thinking that he knew best. The way he wouldn't just leave her alone. The way he didn't take no for an answer.

The djinn's proposed deal had reminded me of Lysander, the ridiculously handsome blond with carving-knife cheek-bones. He had dangled a similar carrot over me, a flash drive that purportedly contained all the data I've ever wanted on my parents, our family home, and my own birth, name, and childhood details I never got to learn. It was the thing I wanted most. I craved that knowledge the way a drought-blasted country craves rain, but I couldn't make the deal. Couldn't give the Silvano Clan what they desired. But the joke was on me, because they got what they wanted in the end, and I still didn't know my last name. I still had to go by my Copperfield-appointed chess piece name they awarded to orphans in their care. I still had to rely on my fuzzy childhood memories to picture what my parents looked like, what their voices sounded like. I didn't even know where their bodies were buried. The pain of that was one thing, but it was overlaid with my feelings of utter self-disgust when I thought of what happened between Lysander and I, which made me even angrier. When I thought of that night I had tried the Vampire Venom, I cringed so hard inside I worried that my conscience would swallow me whole. A bitter black veil descended over me, impossible to shake.

I activated the night vision function on my helmet's visor and accelerated into the dark, knowing that riding on the city streets that night was a terrible idea, and not caring. Perhaps it was the promise of freedom in death that Alif had alluded to. I had always struggled so hard to stay alive, but what if I had it wrong? Maybe death was underrated. Maybe I was right about the Afterlife being like Halloween Heaven. Maybe death was a holiday.

THE OUTSKIRTS of the city seemed calmer than I expected, but as I got closer to the CBD things started to look pretty bad. I guessed that the quietness before was due to people staying home, worried about being out in the open when the Hammerskin orcs were on the rampage. As I neared the center I began to smell the fire and the panic. Rubbish bins had been overturned, so there was garbage strewn everywhere. Some of the storefronts were smashed in, and broken glass littered the pavement. Pedestrians hurried to their destinations. There was no bling, no chatting, no stopping to grab a cheap burger from one of the kiosks on the way.

After hitting three green lights in a row, something made me slow down. There was a shape lying in the road. A body. It wasn't blocking my way—I could have swerved—but instead I slowed down and stopped. There were no cars, and no people. The night air crackled with danger.

You're crazy, I had told the deadling. Talk about the pot calling the kettle black.

I cut the engine, but remained on the bike.

It could be a trap, I told myself. I waited a while, searching for signs of danger, then I tightened the belt on my coat and steeled myself, slowly easing off the bike. I crept up to the body, looking left and right for possible attackers, but there was no one there. Just litter being pushed along the pavements by the bitter breeze, like post-apocalyptic tumbleweed. There was the sourness of city smoke in the air, and shards of glass crunched under my boots.

"Hello?" I said to the inanimate body lying in the road.

I swallowed hard and took a few more steps toward him. The quiet was eerie, and for a second I felt like I was in a gray-colored dream. I reached the orc-sized body, and the streetlight above us flashed and popped, and it became dark around us. I crouched down and rolled the dead body over so that I could see his face. I flinched. It was a Khargol loyalist, and his eyes had been taken.

WHEN I GOT to my apartment building I saw Lou standing on the corner, like she always does, as if the Neo-Nazis weren't prowling the city; burning and killing and gouging out their enemies' eyes.

"Are you insane?" I hissed at her.

Not long ago she had reminded me that I was not invincible, and now I felt as if I should return the favor. Except that maybe she was invincible. With a subtle angling of her body she showed me the djinn blade she kept sheathed, hidden on her back, and I was reminded of the time she walked into the old abandoned chapel and beheaded vampires as if they were baddies in a Samurai video game.

"I can take care of myself," Lou said, looking into the distance.

"I know," I said. "But why chance it? No one's buying spike tonight."

"You'd be surprised," she said. "At times like this, people need a way to escape."

I guess there was no arguing with that.

"But a gang might come along," I said. "And you know what they did to you last time."

Her skin was still not fully healed, and there were some fading bruises on her cheek and jaw. The vulnerable pink skin of her lip had only just mended. The word *gang* echoed in my ears, sounding wrong. What was the collective noun for a group of Neo-Nazi orcs?

"That's because they caught me off-guard," she said. "I wasn't expecting them to attack me. That won't happen again."

"Come up to my place," I said. "We can have a drink."

I wouldn't have minded an hour of escapism, either. Usually I preferred my own company, but waiting alone for Darick to be released would be a whole lot easier if I had a bottle of blitz and someone to share it with. Plus, I was unsettled by my meeting with the deadling. All kinds of questions were flooding into my head.

"I have cinnamon whisky," I said. "*Copper Cog.*"

Lou looked at the empty streets, gazed at the trash can that was burning in the distance, then she looked at me. One eye the color of a river stone, the other bright quinine.

"All right," she said, and we walked to the entrance together.

CHAPTER 23

LIMBO LAND

"So, what do you need?" Lou asked me as we sat down with Ferra's aromatic home-distilled whisky.

I took a sip and it blazed down my throat and warmed my insides. I shook my hair out of my face and leaned my head back. "What do you mean?" I asked.

"I mean, you clearly need something, or I wouldn't be sitting here."

"Not true," I said.

"Isn't it?"

"Okay," I said. "I needed company, and I thought you needed a safe place."

"Ha," said Lou. "You think this place is safe?"

As if on cue, there was a knock at the front door. It was Gnor, my Khargol orc security guard.

"Hey, Gnor, what's up?" I asked. What I really meant was: *what are you doing up?* The man was either chronically exhausted or a champion narcoleptic. There was a reason his name rhymed with *snore*.

Gnor looked ashamed. He stared at the cheap floor tiles.

"I'm Khargol," he said. "In my blood. Always."

"Yes," I said. "I know."

"Hammerskins killing Khargol Familia. Kill every Khargol in SubRealm. Even children."

I started to understand what he was saying. Jo'burg wasn't safe for Khargol loyalists anymore. He wanted to leave town.

"Bad time to leave you," he said. "But need to protect family." He pulled a well-worn wallet out of his back pocket and opened it, showing me a picture. At first I thought, *Why does Gnor have a picture of baby cucumbers rounded up and wrapped in pastrami?* But then I realized they were his children. There were seven of them, and they were all equally aesthetically challenged. They had faces only a mama pickle could love.

Don Vito Or'Capone was dead, the Boss was dead, and the Hammerskins were seizing control. Any Khargol loyalist deciding to stay in Jozi was either too brave, or too stupid.

"Of course you can go," I said. Not that he was asking my permission. I rooted in my coat pocket for my envelope of Farzad's cash, and gave him half of the contents. He smiled at me for the first time, showing off his mossy tombstones in all their halitosis-scented glory, and grunted in thanks.

"Go well," I said, and watched as he stomped into the lift, then closed and bolted the door. I had the feeling I'd never see him again.

"THERE ARE some things I wanted to talk to you about," I said to Lou. Because I never went to wizard conferences and didn't hang out with the Jo'burg Spell of Wizards, I didn't really have many people I could discuss magical matters with. The djinn drug dealer helped herself to another glass of whisky and put her feet up. "I'm listening."

"A friend of mine—a goblin—is missing. She disappeared while she was portaling to a pocket realm to help Darick find Gizmo."

Gizmo squeaked in my pocket. I had forgotten he was sleeping in there.

"Nilve SaltySnap has the strongest Portal Magic I know," I said. "But somehow, she got lost. That doesn't make any sense, does it?"

"Nope," said Lou, shaking her head. "Are you sure she's lost?"

"Yes," I said. "Darick told me what happened."

Lou snorted. "That stalker."

I was about to jump to his defense, but then I remembered the shadow that flitted over Darick's face when we had last discussed Salty's disappearance. I had thought at the time that he was hiding something.

"She wasn't at Goblin City," I said. "She's been reported as officially missing."

"If a goblin who is brilliant at gateway magic disappears while portaling ... I'd say that she *wanted* to get lost."

"But why?"

"Who knows?" asked Lou. "Why do a handful of random people always disappear during terrorist attacks and natural disasters? I guess they have their reasons."

"I was thinking I should portal to her," I said. "I have a portal key now."

"But where will you portal to?"

"I don't know. Maybe Gizmo can lead me to her."

"Do you have anything of the goblin's? A personal possession?"

I was about to shake my head but then I remembered the Goblin City hotel access card she had given me. I pulled it out and showed Lou, who shook her head.

"No way," she said. "Too dangerous."

"What do you mean?"

"That card could have belonged to anyone. She could have nicked it off a colleague's desk. The last thing you want is to accidentally portal to a goblin limbo land."

I imagined being in that video game again, a goblin-themed one.

What was up with me and video games lately?

I had my gold coin points from before, and a magical ferret in my pocket. I imagined Qwynkle and his awkwardly dressed goblin gang going after me, and I'd have to fight them with my pixelated blue magic while they shot at me with Qwynkle's peg-leg. I imagined fighting them, and escaping from them, only to be captured and gobbled up by the gray-skinned goblin.

"I guess so," I said, disappointed. "I'll have to think of something else."

LOU STRETCHED her arms as if she was getting ready to leave, but I still had questions. Kresnik had not yet returned from the Farzad home.

"Do you know anything about breaking a witch's hex?"

Lou frowned at me. "What kind of hex?"

"That psycho," I said. "Ophelia Knox. Bron saw her kill Shackleton in the woods, so she hexed him to stay in his raven form, so he couldn't talk."

She looked at me for a moment, thinking. "That's a tough one," she said. "There're so many different kinds of shifter spells, so many layers of magic. Infinite variations. It's like trying to break the code on a combination lock."

My heart sank. "So ... it's impossible?" I asked.

"Not impossible. Not if you know the spell they cast in the first place."

"In other words, only Ophelia Knox will be able to change him back to Bron."

"Yep," she said. "That sounds about right."

My chest ached for Bron, cursed to live out his life as a raven … unless I could find Ophelia.

"There's one last thing," I said, topping up our tumblers. "A new client of mine. He's a djinn. I thought you could offer some insight."

Lou rolled her eyes and sighed. "Djinn are a dime a dozen. You can't step out of your front door nowadays without bumping into a djinni. What do you need to know?"

"He's a deadling."

Lou's eyebrows shot up. "That's a little more interesting."

"His wife is alive. She's pregnant."

Lou frowned and sat up. "Did she conceive before or after he died?"

"Half-died," I said. "After."

"Ha," she said, tapping her feet. "Interesting."

"I didn't know deadlings could do that," I said.

Lou shook her head. "They can't. But apparently deadling *djinns* can."

"He wants to turn her, so they can be together, but she's afraid for the baby."

"She should be more afraid for herself," Lou said, taking a sip.

"What do you mean?"

"The child will be fine. He or she will be a deadling. But a living person can't give birth to a deadling without, well ... dying."

"That's really confusing," I said. I thought of Samantha Farzad and her huge belly and haunted face.

"She'll die in childbirth," said Lou. "She's in trouble. When is her due date?"

I shrugged. "I don't know. Yesterday. Last week."

Lou pulled a face. "I hope they paid you in advance."

CHAPTER 24
BLACK SPIDERWEB

I said goodbye to Lou at the door. Before I slid the stubborn bolt open, she stopped me and shot me an apologetic look.

"I'm going to pull a *Gnor*," she said.

"What do you mean? Drool in your sleep all day and then dislocate my shoulder?"

"What?"

"Never mind," I said, shrugging it off. "You had to be there."

"He dislocated your shoulder?"

"It's a long story," I said. "What did you mean?"

Lou looked at me, her mismatched eyes flaring. "I'm leaving town."

"No," I said. "Oh, no."

My abandonment issues reared their ugly snake heads, like Medusa's viper-nest hair. It wasn't easy for me to make friends, and now it felt like I was actively repelling them, like a magical magnet that pushed people away. Salty was missing, Darick was still in custody, and now Lou was leaving town.

"I recommend you do the same," she said. "The Realm ain't gonna be a pretty place to live."

"I can't leave," I said. "Everyone I love,"—I could count them on the fingers of one hand—"Everyone I love is here."

"They'll kill you," said Lou. "Those Hammerskins don't have a bone of empathy or mercy in their bodies. They'll kill all of you."

"Don't sugarcoat it," I joked, but Lou didn't smile. Instead she took the silver chain from around her neck and took the blue jewel off it. It was the same color as her quinine eye, and set in silver.

"It's a djinn stone," she said, putting it into my palm. "If you ever need me, you know what to do."

I inspected the beautiful gem, and then clipped it to my charm bracelet, next to the ugly silver star from Darick, the spent bullet he found resting in my heart.

"Thank you," I said. Lou nodded and adjusted her hood, then turned and walked away.

. . .

AFTER SHE LEFT I felt incredibly lonely, and worried. I tried to call Samantha Farzad, but she didn't answer. Plus, I was anxious about Salty. She had been missing for days now; surely if she wanted to be lost she could have at least texted me? I also had to check on Ferra, to make sure her family was okay at *The Copper Cog & Ale,* and that there had been no further attacks. I felt overwhelmed, which made me want to jump into bed and hide under the covers, but then my phone rang, and Morgan sounded panicked.

"Jax," she said. "We're in trouble."

"Tell me about it," I said.

"Don't be a smart-ass," she said. "I'm being serious. Your boyfriend is gone."

"Gone?" I asked, my heart immediately doubling its pace. "Released early?" My voice was high.

"That's what I thought, after that Judge Valar debacle."

I kept quiet, not knowing if the line was secure and not wanting to implicate her. "He's not in SubT?" I asked. She had already said that Darick was gone, but I was trying to wrap my head around it.

"Not in SubT," she said. "And there's no paperwork to say he should be anywhere else."

"Filius Canis," I said. "Musubarin went ahead with the transfer, didn't he? He ignored Valar and went ahead with the *faexing* transfer."

"I hate it when you swear in Latin," Morgan said.

"I know."

"I'm not sure what to say," said Morgan. "If he's been transferred to the Black Tower..."

She didn't finish her sentence. She didn't have to. I felt like screaming and kicking, and throwing the phone across the room. I was more furious with Tilexon Musubarin at that moment than I had ever been with anyone else in my life.

"I am so angry I can't think straight," I said, and I felt as if I was literally steaming. "What do I do?"

"There's nothing you can do," said Morgan. "Those maximum security transfers are totally locked down. Mechanically, technologically, magically. There's no way you'd be able to stop it."

I was desperate. "I'll go see Musubarin," I said.

Morgan guffawed. "You're crazy. Don't you know that he has a very unhealthy obsession with you? Like, he'll die a very happy man if he can finally arrest you. Which is exactly what he'll do if you approach him."

"I'll appeal to his better nature," I said.

"Tilexon Musubarin doesn't have a better nature."

"I'll exchange my freedom for Darick's. That's what he wants, anyway, isn't it?"

"And what help would that be?" asked Morgan. "Then Darick would be trying to get you out and it would just be a silly game of musical chairs."

Musical Chairs: the Maximum Security Edition.

"Would you let me into the Scorpion HQ?" I asked. "If I came over now?"

"Of course I would. But Moose isn't here. He's taken the squad on some kind of team building stunt at *Laser Dungeon.*"

You're not part of the squad? I wanted to ask. And then I remembered the argument Musubarin and Morgan had earlier. *Not anymore,* she would have replied, and in my mind Kim Smith's witness statement burned and burned on my kitchen table, and my guilt was the acrid smoke in the air.

"I'll call Valar," I said.

"Judge Valar doesn't take calls from wily girl wizards."

"I'll get Blimaex to call her."

"She doesn't take calls from wily old man wizards, either. I can't imagine how Tilexon got her in here this afternoon."

"It's because it wasn't him," I said.

"What?"

"It wasn't him who got her to come in. I bet you it was the Council. I don't know what's going on, but they're up to something."

"Jax," said Morgan, sounding stern. "Don't get confused. The Council are on our side. The good side. Right?"

"Right," I said. No matter how strangely they were behaving, every pillar of the Council was a wizard beyond reproach.

They knew a lot more than we did. Their entire reason for being was to serve and protect the Realm.

"Then, in that case, you've got to ask yourself, why would the Council want Darick incarcerated?"

My anger dissipated and was replaced with dread. I closed my eyes and tried to quieten my mind. What was I missing? Was I so blinded by whatever it was that I felt for Darick that I couldn't see who he truly was? What was he hiding from me? I hated this self-doubt, this not knowing.

But there was one true thing, and that was how I felt when I was with Darick. I connected with him on such a deep and intense level; it was a feeling I'd never experienced before. My uncertainty paled in comparison to the strength of my feelings for him. I was just going to have to believe in what my heart was telling me, which made me even more scared, because it meant that I had to find him and set him free.

"Where do I even start?" I asked.

"Start what?" Morgan asked. "There's nothing you can do."

"There must be something. And you have to help me."

"Jax," Morgan said, and I imagined her scrunching her eyes closed and scratching her forehead with the back of her pen. "I'm up for a disciplinary hearing tomorrow morning."

Oh hex, I thought. *I had forgotten about her demotion.*

"Darick's case file was in my office," she said. "And an important piece of evidence grew a pair of legs."

Yikes.

"I'm being questioned about it tomorrow. I don't think I'll be wearing a badge when I walk out of that hearing."

I imagined that smoke from the burning testimony swirling around me, tangling me up, stinging my lungs.

"They wouldn't," I said.

Morgan laughed; a short, bitter cough. "Oh yes, they would."

"I owe you a drink," I said. "Somewhere quiet. How about tomorrow?"

I hoped that she would read between the lines, and know that I meant I'd tell her everything when we next had the chance.

She sighed loudly. "That's the best thing I've heard all day. But what are you going to do now? I have a distinct sense of foreboding that you're about to do something reckless."

"Who, me?" I said, as innocently as I could. There would be nothing to gain by telling her my plan. I pulled my trench coat on and clipped the crossbow to my back.

"Jacquelyn Denna Knight," she said. "Please be careful."

CHAPTER 25

THE LASER DUNGEON

"Gizmo," I whispered into my pocket. "Wake up. I need your help."

Gizmo's eyes snapped open, and then he had a full-body stretch that showed off his soft, snowy belly. It reminded me of those furry pillows you see in shop windows at the spice-fragrant Oriental Plaza.

"I need to go to *Laser Dungeon*," I said. Luckily I had a Skeleton Portal Key, and a magical albino ferret with a special talent for finding things.

He nodded and pawed his whiskers. I wondered where Bron was, and couldn't help worrying about him. I guess if you have wings, you don't want to hang around on a wizard's shoulder all day. I still needed to find some way to break that hex. It was one of my ninety-nine problems, ninety-eight of which I couldn't address at that very moment.

The underhanded transfer of Darick to the Ember Isles was my top priority. I wasn't going to let a substandard wizard with an ego take Darick away from me, and I certainly wasn't going to let Darick die in some dim, dank prison cell at the hands of some overenthusiastic ogre with boulder-knuckled fists and a shallow EQ. Everyone in the Realm knows that it's impossible to break out of the Bermuda Triangle that is Ember Island, so that was not an option. I needed to reach Darick before he was delivered, or die trying.

Samantha Farzad was second on my fires-to-put-out list, but she wasn't answering calls, and my texts came back undelivered. I was worried about her, but I didn't have time to go over there.

I STOOD with the portal key in my hands, and imagined Musubarin at the *Laser Dungeon*.

"Ianua Sit," I said, and I felt the warmth of the key immediately, and the manic golden butterflies. The power of the key pulled my body into separate blocks again, 3D pixels, and the little wizard-flavored cubes were swept away—an exploding Rubik's Cube—and flew through a buzzing tunnel of bronze and gray. Usually I like to watch the vertigo-inducing trip, but I closed my eyes and prepared myself for battle, instead. Tilexon Musubarin was a stubborn *fillius canis*, and I needed to get information out of him. Add to that the thirty or so officers he'd have with him, and all of a sudden I was agreeing with Morgan when she had called me crazy. I didn't beat myself up about it; I was sure there were plenty of Musubarin's men who'd happily oblige. I patted my silver wand and flexed my fingers to warm them up.

Let the games begin.

~

THE PORTAL MAGIC DUMPED ME, quite unceremoniously, into a dumpster in an alley.

I heard a loud "*OOF!*," and I wasn't sure if it came from me or the homeless person I had landed on. I apologized and climbed out, finger-combing my hair to remove any stray plastic wrappers or sauce-smeared napkins, but I couldn't get rid of the rancid smell of the rubbish. *Smooth,* I thought, as I pulled a price tag off the back of my thigh. Apparently I was currently marked down to a dollar, at R14.99.

I was about to scold Gizmo for getting us lost, and make him feel ashamed with my disappointed-mama eyes, but then I looked up and saw that what I thought was an alley was really a stage setup. The brick wall was made of painted board, and the road was a kind of black rubber mat. When I peered into the dumpster again, I saw that the homeless person I had landed on was just a discarded dummy.

WHEN I HAD FIRST HEARD of *Laser Dungeon* it had been a small outfit in an actual dungeon. The concept was to have a kind of *Dungeons & Dragons* in real time, with magic. That's where the laser tag comes in (and the fae, witches, orcs, trolls, goblins, dwarfs, and wizards).

As the popularity of the game grew, the dungeon was no longer big enough, and they expanded from the original basement of the teen CEO's parents' house into a disused part of the SubRealm not inhabited by orcs. Now there was an ants' nest of a subterranean micro-city built here, with various themes and concepts according to what you may enjoy as a customer. There's the original magical creatures area, which is where most of the action takes place, and then there are places like this, where I was standing, which looked like a ghost town. Or, rather, the replica of a ghost town.

They called the various areas "cats" as in "categories." There were cats and sub-cats, which I guess was confusing for first-time visitors, because *Laser Dungeon's* Forage advertising were forever boasting about how many new cats they had on the block.

If a customer wanted a vampire-based game, they'd go to the Vampire cat, and from there it was possible to further ensnare oneself: X-rated Steamy Vamp; Vampire Slayer; and Blood Lust were just some of the sub-cats available. Of course, if I were playing, my first choice would always be to ash some vampires.

By portaling in, instead of using the regular entrance, I had skipped the admission counter, the steep ticket price, and the tools I'd need to fit in down here. By gatecrashing what-ever sub this was I had made myself extremely vulnerable, because the Scorpions would all be wearing their *Laser Dungeon* custom-designed glamours, protective gear, and NGA-approved weapons, while all I had was a trash-scented trench coat. I had my wand and crossbow, too, of course, but, for obvious reasons, you weren't allowed to use real magic down there. The weapons they give you act like the real thing, but no one gets hurt. Fake magic. Paranormal paint-ball. If their sensors detect real magic you're hauled out before you can say *lethal damage.*

So I didn't have a glamour, and I was probably going to be outnumbered fifty to one. But I've beaten worse odds before —the volcano pocket realm and the *Olde Worlde Railway* trap sprang to mind—so I thought I was in with a fighting chance. Suddenly, there was a zapping sound behind me. A current of red lifted me a meter in the air and then slammed me to the ground.

So much for fake magic.

CHAPTER 26
SHATTERED SPIDERWEB

Despite being in shock, I managed to reach for my wand and grab it while I spun onto my back and pointed it at my attacker. A demon with an ebony skull and black horns on his head growled at me. In his hands was a snake-headed staff.

"You're not supposed to use real magic down here, you cretin," I said, my knees still hurting from the fall.

The demon roared at me, and it came out in a blast of red smoke that stung my ears and eyes at the same time. He was a black skeleton under his heavy cloak, and his red eyes were lasers on my skin. It was a pretty convincing glamour. I wondered who the person was, underneath. I also wondered how long it would take the powers that be at *Laser Dungeon* to send their security guards down to turf this guy out. Their magic sensors must have picked that blast up; if it was strong enough to raze me like it did, it must have registered on their system. I figured it would take them a couple of minutes at the most, so all I had to do was stay alive till then. Easier said than done, when you're blinded by red smoke.

The skeleton began walking towards me—in that jerky way skeletons do—and was about to roar again. I couldn't handle another blast of acidic air; my lungs were already protesting, and my eyes were streaming. He lifted his staff and sent a hot current of magenta magic my way, and I rolled away from it. It smoked the floor mat where I had been lying.

To hex with it, I thought. If he was going to use magic, so would I. Maybe it would get the guards down here faster. I used my a floor jump to get off the ground and pointed my wand at the demon.

"Nano, mask," I said, and my nano climbed out of my pocket and clamped over my face in a hard black shell. My eyes stopped stinging, and I could breathe. If I could see, and I could breathe, I could fight.

"Fiat fulgar!" I shouted, and a fireball left my wand and barreled towards the demon. It glanced off his shoulder and made him roar again, and he sent another bolt of magic my way. I ducked just in time, and the purple-flamed fire incinerated the cardboard brick wall behind me.

I had to keep in mind that it wasn't a real demon. There was a humanoid underneath that glamour, so best I didn't annihilate the guy, even if he seemed intent on killing me. This was supposed to be a game, but I didn't think the authorities would see it that way if a dead body turned up.

Where were the security guards? They should have been here by now.

Usually I wouldn't run away from a fight, but I didn't see the point in finishing this one. Skeletor roared again and lifted his staff, but before he could send another current my way I skittered behind the burning wall and into the next alley. The demon followed me.

I RACED away from the black skeleton, dodging the meteor-storm of destructive magic he was sending my way. He was clumsy and had an awkward gait, so I was able to gain some ground. The fake walls, rocks and trees that he exploded around me made me feel like I was in some kind of dream. I was in this weird half-baked reality where a demon had it in for me. I didn't really understand what I was doing there but I knew I had to trust Gizmo. He had never let me down.

I was sweating under my mask, and my legs were burning. I needed to find my way out of there. Then I saw the camou-flaged elevator, painted in the same red-brick pattern as the walls. The doors were already closing, so I had to take a running jump to make it. I leapt into the air and only just slid through the gap, falling hard against the opposite mirrored wall and the steel plate of the floor. I bashed my head on the mirror so hard I heard it crack. The demon bellowed and clamoured outside, but not in time. The elevator door closed. It began to rise, leaving the skeleton behind.

As I opened my eyes I saw my fractured reflection in the jagged wall-mirror. I wondered if my skull looked the same, under my swelling scalp. A shattered spiderweb. And then all poetic thoughts of injury left me in a whoosh of air escaping from my lungs, because I saw movement in the cracked mirror, and I realized I wasn't alone.

CHAPTER 27

GLAMOUR GUNS BLAZING

"I didn't figure you for a *Laser Dungeon* kind of wizard," said a familiar voice. It wasn't friendly.

I blinked past the stars in my head. Could the day get any more surreal? Where were the vampire strippers, the werewolf cubs, the rainbow orcs? I was waiting for the elevator to blow up in a glitter bomb and people would yell, "*Surprise! We were Just Kidding! That red-laser-eyed demon was the perfect touch, right?*"

But there were no strippers, vampire or otherwise, and no glitter. Only a wizard standing in the corner of the elevator, his wand at the ready.

"How very convenient," he said.

Of course, he didn't look like a wizard, because he was wearing a *Laser Dungeon (TM)* glamour, but I would have recognized his voice anywhere. The magical costume didn't fool me, even though I was sure I had lost at least one hundred IQ points when my head slammed into the mirror.

Vomit pushed up my throat, but I was able to keep it down. Was it the beginning of a concussion, or did the thought of sharing an enclosed space with this man make me feel ill? Probably a bit of both. I stood up and steadied myself, dizzy and sick.

I looked at the creature, a troll with a rough skin and a runny nose. His rubbery lips smacked and leered. He had around a dozen hairs plastered to his dirty head, and the rest was a greasy, flaky sphere. His appearance was despicable in every way.

"Your glamour really suits you," I said.

"Ha," he said, and a large glob of saliva trickled from his slimy mouth to the floor.

"You're under arrest," he said.

"Bite me," I said.

It was a manner of speech, of course. If you saw the state of the troll's teeth, you would submit to being arrested before being bitten every day of the week and twice on Sundays.

The elevator came to a stop, and the doors pinged and slid open. Ground floor. At least we were far away from the demon below, who I imagined was gnashing his black teeth and trying to tear the elevator doors open.

"After you," said Musubarin, gesturing for me to leave first.

"No," I said, politely. I even managed a tight smile. "I insist."

We stood there, each stubbornly refusing to move, and the doors closed again, but the lift stayed still.

"Why are you so intent of getting rid of Darick?" I asked.

"I've always thought that his name has a bit of a vampiric ring to it," said Musubarin. "Don't you think so?"

I ignored the jibe. It was getting old. "You know he's innocent," I said. "Why the push to get him to the Ember Isles?"

"I'm sure you know the answer to that," he said.

"Revenge?" I said. "To get back at me?"

The troll laughed, splattering the floor with clear slime. "Despite what you may think, Jacquelyn Denna Knight, the Realm does not revolve around you."

What can I say? Sometimes it felt like it did.

"Then why?" I asked. "Why ship an innocent man off to a certain death?"

"There are things you don't know," said Musubarin.

My anger flared, and I bunched my fingers into fists. "I'm getting so sick and tired of hearing that."

The troll eyed me with his bulging glassy orbs, bloodshot and twitching.

"More specifically, then," he sneered. "There are things about Darick Noble that you don't know."

I shoved my wand into his face. "Then tell me!" I said.

He laughed again, and I narrowly escaped being spat on. An umbrella would have come in handy right then.

"I'll tell you everything you need to know," he said. With a click of his fingers, a pair of handcuffs snapped onto my right wrist and the handrail of the elevator, locking me in place. I looked down and swore under my breath. Musubarin was so good at that particular trick. It was the second time he had caught me.

"I'll tell you everything you need to know when I have you locked up safely in a cell."

I rattled the steel cuffs against the glass. Musubarin looked pleased with himself.

"I've been working on that spell," he said.

He was so smug I felt like kicking him in the gonads again, but then I had a better idea. While he looked away from me and spoke into the microphone on his watch to alert his team, I placed my palm on the rail, as if I was leaning on it.

Ignem Exquiris, I chanted in my head, as loudly and clearly as I could. *Ignem Exquiris. Ignem Exquiris.* I directed my spell towards the screws that kept the rail fastened to the wall.

Slowly, the screws began to glow orange. The metal beneath my palm became warm, and then hot. The troll was too busy giving orders to see what I was doing. It got hotter and hotter, and I let go just before it had the chance to burn me.

The elevator door pinged again, and began to open. That was my cue. With all the strength I could muster, I pulled my handcuffed arm away from the wall, and the softened screws lost their traction and stripped. Musubarin's face registered shock and then determination as he pointed his wand at me and began to stutter a spell. With a final wrench, the rail came off. I grabbed it with both hands and slammed it into Musubarin's swollen, greasy face. It burnt my hands, and I gasped and let it go, letting it clang to the floor. The troll physique is tough, so I thought it would take more than one blow to take him down. But of course he was just an ordinary human underneath the convincing disguise. After I brained Musubarin as hard as I could, I realized that, with such a blow, I could have killed the captain of the Scorpions.

MUSUBARIN CRIED out in pain and he immediately lost consciousness. His body drooped to the floor. As he sagged, I slid my cuff off the end of the pole. Then I searched his revolting tunic and almost immediately found what I was looking for.

Handcuff keys: one gold point.

One Laser Dungeon access card: one hundred gold points.

I could practically feel the animated 3D coin spinning above my head. I couldn't let that distract me, though, because I was pretty sure I had less than a minute to find what I was looking for and get out of there before Musubarin's men appeared. I slipped the cuffs into my pocket. Stealing two pairs of handcuffs in one day pointed to the fact that I probably had a problem, but I didn't let it bother me too much. I quite liked the crisp irony of it all.

. . .

I LEFT Musubarin's troll-shaped body in the elevator and sent it down to the floor with the angry smoke-spilling skeleton, then I raced towards the locker rooms. The number on the access card led me around two corners and then to a tall blue locker, which beeped with a green light before I even showed it the card. The painted metal door swung open, revealing Musubarin's military-style backpack, which I grabbed and unzipped. I found his gun, his wallet and his laptop.

Eleventy thousand gold points!

I imagined the sound of a slot machine payout and coins clattering into a metal catch tray, but my nerves soon took over and it faded to an anxious hum. I quickly opened the laptop, wanting to search for any details he may have on Darick's transfer. Of course, a password prompt appeared, instead, and I realized I wouldn't have time to try to work it out before the officers arrived, glamour guns blazing. I hadn't planned to steal Musubarin's bag, but I was out of time. I closed it, zipped it back up, and slung it over my shoulder. I took out my portal key and uttered the gateway spell, and as the sound of boots arrived in the locker room, my vision exploded into silver sparks and I fell down and away into my gray vacuum gateway.

CHAPTER 28
CYMBAL-CLASHING CIRCUS MONKEYS

I didn't have a location in mind when I used the portal key, which is usually a dangerous idea. Luckily Gizmo directed us home. The first thing I did was look out of my window, down at the noisy streets below. The city was, as expected, still in upheaval. People of all species walked the litter-strewn streets with faces bleached by anxiety. They carried weapons: baseball bats; automatic rifles; staffs; tasers. Shop alarms were screeching from all over, their shelves looted and destroyed. Smoke tinted the air gray, hiding the stars. I closed the window again and took Musubarin's laptop to my bed. It was almost midnight and I hadn't slept in days, but I couldn't allow myself to sleep when Darick's life was in danger. I plugged the computer in and started guessing at passwords, which is tricky if you don't really know the person, don't know the name of their first born, or their favorite pet and/or pizza. All I could think of was Musubarin's awful troll face, his bulging eyes, and the feeling of smashing the handrail into his greasy head. I guessed and guessed until my eyes starting crossing. I closed them, just for a quick rest. Just for a minute or two.

I woke up with a start, ten hours later. The sun was blazing, the sky was blue, and my heart started galloping in my chest, terrified. I yanked open Musubarin's laptop and started trying various passwords again.

Moose69

ScOrp1On

TilexON

This time the computer knew I was up to something, and it locked me out after the third attempt. It would only let me try again after ten minutes. I smashed down some keys in frustration and then punched the whole keyboard with my fist.

Filius canis!

Morgan said that the Ember Isles transfers take a minimum of twenty-four hours, because the bus travels across the country to pick up the various convicts. Darick disappeared from the SubT cells at around six p.m. the evening before, and it was just past ten a.m., so I had at least eight hours to find him. Still, I realized it was cutting it close, and my hands started perspiring on the laptop's keyboard. I closed it and slung it to the side. You'd think I'd feel rested after a marathon snooze like that, but my nerves were jangling hard, and I felt it all over my body. It felt as if I had a hundred of those cymbal-clashing circus monkeys inside my brain, and their racket reverberated through my body. I had to calm down or I wouldn't get anywhere.

I felt a cold breeze, and the goblin-sized shower switched itself on. Ghost. I lifted my arms and sniffed my armpits. My B.O. would have made an orc proud. It was settled, then. I'd take a quick shower and then try unlocking the computer again.

My phone has a unique talent. It seems to know exactly the most time to ring, and then doesn't stop. Lonely nights? Not a beep. Feeling like a chat? No signal, no data. Just about to kiss melted-honey-voiced Darick? RI-I-I-I-ING! RING-RING-RING!

In the shower, all lathered up? It rings like there's no tomorrow. My phone just loves it when I shower. It seems to get a new lease on life as soon as I step into the tiny, cracked glass cubicle.

It was the worst phone in the world, I was thinking, as I heard it start buzzing. I got shampoo in my eyes and almost slipped on the wet tiles. I already had a mild concussion from flinging myself against the mirrored wall in the elevator the day before. An extra bump on the head might knock me out for good. It might knock me all the way to Halloween Heaven.

I couldn't look at the caller ID because my eyes were stinging like hell, and I was dripping water everywhere. I hurriedly toweled off my hands, then grabbed the thing, blindly guessing where the green phone icon was. It took me three stabs at the screen to strike it lucky.

"Hello?" I said, my eyeballs still smarting.

"Jinx!" said Ferra. "I need your help."

Ferra never asked for help. Ever. Her dwarf fairy godmother act was usually a one-way street.

I gulped. "Of course," I said, thinking of the time racing away from me, along with the Ember Isles transfer bus. Something told me that if I agreed to help Ferra, I'd never see Darick again. It was a hot spear in my heart.

"Of course, Ferra," I said. "Anything. What do you need?"

CHAPTER 29

EVERY MUSCLE AND EVERY HEARTSTRING

Ferra Fernak was more distraught than I'd ever heard her. Dwarfs are stoic, and Ferra especially so, but I picked up something in her voice that morning that I'd never heard before.

"What is it?" I asked. "What happened?"

"They've taken the *Cog*," said Ferra.

My entire body wilted.

No! I thought. *No, no, no!*

"What do you mean?" I asked, even though I knew exactly what she meant. I needed to hear her say it, as painful as it was, for the reality to sink in. We both knew it had been a matter of time, but the fact that it had really happened was just the most terrible, terrible thing. The lump in my throat grew, and I started to tremble.

By the sounds of things, Ferra was also having trouble keeping the emotion from cutting into her voice. "They arrived at nightfall," she said. "There were three dozen of them, all armed and ready for battle."

"Oh, no," I said, voice thick with tears. I thought of the way Ferra's face was usually lit up by the vintage lanterns that blazed in her glimmering steampunk-themed pub, and the blazing fire in the center of the flagstone floor. The clocks that ticked cheerfully on the exposed brick walls, and the shiny copper piping. The fact that there was always an extra table for any creature of any species or race who visited, and, of course, the fantastic food. Not to mention, behind the kitchen, Ferra's jaw-dropping high-tech lab.

Oh, the cruelty of it, the waste. I imagined the Hammerskins smashing glasses and wasting food, breaking the kitchen equipment and cracking the hearth. I imagined the disgusting orcs sleeping in the Fernaks' bedrooms and lazily lighting their cigars with flaming family photos. It made me feel utterly sick. It made me boil with emotions, from a white fury to a deep, aching grief.

"I'm so sorry for you," I said.

"We fought as hard as we could," said Ferra. "Even the children did. We battled with everything we had, every muscle and every heartstring, but it wasn't enough. Fez was hurt. So was little Frankie, but they're all right now. We're lucky to all be alive." Ferra cleared her throat, then added softly, "It could have ended very differently."

"But where are you now? Can I come to you? Bring you anything? Would you like to come and stay here with me?"

Ferra laughed. "The fourteen of us! In that apartment! Can you imagine what fun and games that would be, now? No, thank you for the offer, Jinxie, but we've settled in to our new home very nicely."

"What?" I asked. "Where?"

"You know, Fig always laughs at me for stocking up the basement the way I do," the dwarf said. "But basements are ideal shelters for dwarfs. The ceilings are the right height, for one. Everything is within reach."

"You're in the basement?" I asked. "At *The Cog*?"

"The Hammerskins are stomping around right above us," said Ferra. "I used a sophisticated security spell on the lock of the trapdoor. Even if they knew we were here, they wouldn't be able to get to us."

"I'll portal to you," I said. "I'll bring you food and water."

The sadness seemed to leave Ferra's voice then, and it was replaced by a spark of mischief. "After those first orcs arrived yesterday, when you were here, I got the skunks to move all the food down here—believe me, there's more than enough —and all the most important things. We've got Fig's flatscreen, my back-up drives, toys for the children. Beds and blankets. It's very cozy. And you know how I like to preserve food for a rainy day," she said.

"Yes," I said. "I do." Ferra had been preserving blushing apricots in almond-flavored syrup, curried kidney beans, rosy apples, rhubarb ginger marmalade, honeyed purple figs, and a host of other things for as long as I had known her. Fighour used to joke that she could feed the entire Realm for a good few years, with all the food and cider she had on hand.

Nonsense, she used to say, and punch him on the shoulder. *Not at the rate you eat, anyway.*

"But I do need a favor," Ferra said.

"Anything."

A violence rose inside me. I wanted to go over there and annihilate those thieving brutes. I wanted to put bolts in their chests.

"It's Pip and Eafy," she said, and I felt a new rush of cold dread. The Belore twins had been through more than enough trauma in their short lives. I felt suddenly fiercely protective of them. If a Hammerskin so much as touched a hair on either of their heads I'd smash them into an early grave.

"Are they at Copperfield?" I asked.

"For now."

"What does that mean?"

"Directress Copperfield called. They're closing the school until things have stabilized."

Closing the school? That had never happened in the century the Institute had been open.

"The orcs are moving above ground for total control. It's just a matter of time before they annex the hostel at the Copperfield Institute. The directress asked us to collect the twins, but we're ... not going anywhere."

"I'll go and get them right away," I said.

The Copperfield Institute lay in the opposite direction to the Ember Isles, so I would *really* have to move it. I shifted the phone away from my mouth and took a deep breath.

You're kidding yourself, said a rather unpleasant (but sensible) voice in my head. *You'll never be able to do both. You have to choose between the Belore twins and Darick.*

But that was an impossible decision, and I refused to make it. I'd get Eafaris and Pepin, deliver them to Ferra at *The Copper Cog* basement, and then race to find Darick.

I PULLED some clothes on in record speed and grabbed Musubarin's laptop. I slung it into his backpack, wondering vaguely as I zipped it up if he had made it out of the *Laser Dungeon* alive.

Looking back, it seemed to me to be excessively convenient that he had been in that elevator ... as if he had been expecting me to arrive. Had he purposefully told Morgan that he would be there, knowing she would pass the message on to me? Had he somehow arranged for that starveling demon to corner me, knowing the only way out was that particular elevator? And is that why the security guards never arrived, and Musubarin was alone, instead of "team building" with his squad?

I checked my crossbow and my wand, and wondered how Samantha Farzad was. I pictured her straining belly, and the baby inside her, and I hoped the grub would stay put till I was able to meet with her again, or the next time I'd see her haunted face would be at her funeral.

Stay put, Baby, I thought. *Stay cozy. No need to rush out into this mad, bad world.*

If only the woman would pick up her phone. As usual, I needed to be in three different places at once, and I thought, not for the first time, that I should try my hand a cloning potion. It was just a joke, of course. Everyone knows that cloning potions don't work the way they should. It's about the third law of thermodynamics, or something like that.

I was reminded of a creased and faded motivational poster that hung from the wall in the Goblin City hotel admin office when I broke in to access their mainframe. I had plenty of time to stare at it while I was averting my eyes from Polkadot and KandyKane's hobnobbing Olympics.

It always seems impossible until it's done, said the headline.

Well, I thought, clutching the portal key in my hands. *It was time to do the impossi—*

Then the doorbell rang. I froze. I couldn't afford a distraction. I needed to speed over to the twins. I didn't have time to answer it, but a plume of cold air on my neck told me that I had to.

CHAPTER 30
STREET SPLASHES

I wanted to ignore the doorbell. I had to get to the Belore twins ASAP, and then somehow find Darick. But the ringing was insistent, and I had the distinct feeling that Ghost wanted me to answer the door. When I got closer I heard a woman cry out in pain, so I had no choice. I wrenched it open.

Samantha Farzad stood in my doorway. She was groaning and crying, clutching her huge pregnant belly.

Oh no, I thought. *Oh, no no no.*

She looked at me, desperately pale. "Please help me."

"Samantha!" I said. "You should be in a hospital! What are you doing here?"

"I need your help," she said. "I didn't have anywhere else to go."

"Hospital!" I yelled. "That's where you should have gone." I was a wizard, for *faex* sake, not a midwife.

She cried out again as a contraction hit, doubling over and leaning against the entrance wall. I moved to support her, putting her arm over my shoulder.

"You need to be at a hospital," I said for the third time. "I'll take you downstairs and put you in a taxi."

Her hair was plastered to her head, perspiration covered her body.

"You haven't been outside today," she said. "There are no taxis. The hospitals are closed."

"There are no taxis?" I said. Then I looked at her legs, which were covered in dust and street splashes. "You walked here?"

Samantha nodded. I could hear that she was trying to keep her breathing under control.

"There must be somewhere, some kind of clinic, open," I said.

She shook her head. "I tried everywhere, till my phone's battery went dead. Then our power was cut. The Hammer-skins blew up the local substation."

Holy Faex, I thought. The orcs would come after our electricity, too, and cut it off. Then they'd cut off our water supply. Samantha groaned again, and I was reminded that I had more immediate problems to deal with.

I can't help you give birth, I thought, but I didn't say it out loud. It seemed cruel and pointless, as the truth often is.

I couldn't help her give birth, but I knew someone who could. I moved Sam to the charity-shop chair, levered her gently into it, and grabbed my phone. Isadora Crowe picked up on the third ring.

"Izzy. It's Jax."

"I wasn't expecting to hear from you again," she said.

There was no time for small talk.

"You're a witch. You know about female rites of passage and things. Witches are descended from midwives, right?"

"What are you talking about?"

"How soon can you get here?" I asked.

Isadora Crowe, High Priestess of the StarDust Coven, arrived in thirteen minutes.

"I brought supplies!" she announced.

Thank the Void, I thought. I was so grateful that it made me wonder why I had ever disliked her.

"How did you get here so quickly?" I asked. As far as I knew, witches didn't portal.

"We've come a long way from the days of straw brooms," she said, and left it at that, which was good, because Samantha's groaning was getting more intense by the moment.

"Shall I boil the kettle or something?" I asked, feeling stupid and totally out of my depth. I didn't even know if I had a kettle anymore. The plant may have eaten it.

"Run a warm bath," she said. "The water will ease the pain."

"I don't have a tub," I said. "Have you seen the size of my bathroom?"

Celestine, the cat, blinked at me. He was the same navy blue as Isadora's witch cloak. I had the feeling he was judging me. It wasn't the first time I had been sized up by a feline and found wanting.

Crowe put him on the floor and her bag on the kitchen counter. It was a small bag, but she managed to pull out all manner of objects, large and small, and there still seemed to be an endless supply waiting. One of the objects was a spotless white tablecloth, which she snapped in the air and let fall perfectly onto the kitchen tabletop. Soon the surface was covered with steel instruments, potions, herbs, stones, and candles. There were white towels, surgical scissors, and a snow-colored receiving blanket. An apron found its way onto Crowe's torso. Seemingly satisfied with the arrangement, she washed her hands with the antibacterial soap she had brought along, then pulled on some latex gloves.

"I can see you've done this before," I said, relieved as anything.

"In fact, I haven't," she said. "But I've watched every episode of Grey's Anatomy. And there were, like, a hundred seasons."

I wanted to laugh and cry at the same time.

"Hey," she said softly, and I looked at her. Crowe's eyes were twinkling. "Hey. I was joking."

"So, you have done this before?"

"Loads of times. Loads," she said, putting her hands on her hips. "Farmyard animals count, right?"

CHAPTER 31
VIOLENT PUDDLE OF BLOOD

Samantha was breathing in the short, focused way you see laboring women do in films before their whole world is ripped open and they start swearing at their husbands. Every now and then a contraction took her and she moaned and growled.

Isadora checked Sam's cervix and then snapped off her gloves. She brought the ticking silver pocket watch out of her cloak and studied its face.

"They're getting really close together," said Crowe. "The baby's head is engaged, and the labor's progressing fast. I think we'll have a baby on our hands in the next twenty minutes."

I gulped. "Would you like to lie down?" I asked Samantha.

The least I could do, I thought, *was make up my bed with clean linen. If there was clean linen.*

"Later," said Crowe. "For now we let gravity do the work."

Of course, when I went to my room, my bed was beautifully made up with sheets that smelled like fabric softener and sunshine, and made me think of my dad, and my mom. I'd never know where I was born, or how the birth went.

I gazed at the perfect bed, feeling tearful. "Thank you, Ghost," I said.

Sam started screaming from the living room, and I raced to her.

What is it? I was about to ask, but then I saw the violent puddle of blood on the floor, and the look on Samantha's face with the shock of it.

"Is there supposed to be so much ... blood?" I asked Crowe, who shook her head. Her lips were clamped together in a worried way. She started to feel Sam's belly, pressing on it to feel where the baby was. Then there was a new pair of gloves on her hands, and another cervix inspection. "Baby's ready, Samantha, and you're fully dilated," she said. "Let's do this."

"Wait!" I said, and both women looked at me as if I was crackers.

"Wait?" said Crowe.

"I have to tell you something."

"*Now* you have to tell me something," said the witch.

"There's something you need to know, about the baby."

"I'm listening," she said.

Samantha shouted in pain, and the contraction seemed to go on for a long time.

"The baby's father is a deadling." I said. "Was already a deadling when the baby was conceived."

"Not possible," said Crowe.

"He's a djinn," I said.

Crowe's face changed as her understanding dawned.

"A deadling djinn?" she asked, and Samantha screamed again, and there was another stream of blood. Crowe checked Sam's pulse rate against her pocket watch, and her face tensed again. "A living woman can't give birth to a deadling," she said. "Not without ..."

Dying.

"I know," I said. "That's why I needed you here. We need to turn her. I don't know how."

Isadora blinked at me. "We can't *turn her*," she said. "That's not our kind of magic."

"But a ... djinn would be able to?" I asked.

"Well, in theory. Yes. But not a deadling djinn."

I knew that Alif wasn't able to turn his wife into a deadling or he would never have had her hire me. Samantha's skin faded to ivory, and her crying became weak. The contractions were still wracking her body. Crowe offered her a cup of water but Sam smacked it out of her hands, then collapsed.

We moved her into my bedroom, and laid her down on my bed.

"Decedere. De vita exire," said Crowe, in the Latin we had learned together at school. It sounded complicated, but it was very simple. *She's dying.*

I looked at the djinn stone on my charm bracelet and rubbed it. We waited, listening to Samantha groan as the life leaked out of her.

JUST AS I was about to give up, there was a crackle in the air, as if the room was suddenly full of charged particles, and then there was the bitter scent of an electric fire. Lou appeared before us, looking mildly irritated. The top of her body looked normal enough, but her legs were swirling smoke.

"I'm not your pizza delivery guy," she said. "I gave you that talisman for emergencies only."

"It's an emergency," said Izzy.

Lou noticed Crowe for the first time. "Oh?" she said.

The two women had met a couple of days before at the Moonlit Chapel, where we had won the fight inside the abandoned church against the Silvano Clan. Crowe had been brilliant with her Death Spell, and Lou was a master with her djinn blade. We strode out of that chapel feeling like battle goddesses; victors no one would ever threaten again. A witch, a wizard, and a djinn. Supernatural Charlie's Angels.

But this situation was different. There was no enemy to fight, just a woman on the leaning ledge of death, and a baby fighting to be born.

Lou understood the situation without any further explanation from me.

"You worry about the baby," she said to Izzy, taking Samantha's limp hand in her smoking one. Crowe nodded and readied herself for the crowning. Lou sent her smoke cascading over Samantha Farzad and began to incant a spell in what sounded like Arabic. I felt the presence of Alif then, too, but I couldn't see him.

Samantha seemed to get a burst of energy, then, and Lou squeezed her hand and encouraged her to push, which she did, shouting out loud with the effort.

"I can see the head!" Izzy shouted.

Lou was whispering magic into Sam's ear, which sustained her. She yelled and pushed again, and her face turned red. The baby crowned.

"Head's out!" said Crowe. "Head's out." And then she breathed out a sigh. I hadn't realized how worried she had been until I saw that look of relief on her face.

Lou kept up the spell casting as the ozone-smelling smoke swirled around us and filled the room. Little orange sparks of electricity buzzed in the air.

"One last push," said Crowe.

Lou nodded, and uttered the final verse, her voice growing louder with each line. The electricity was zapping and popping in the plumes of white. The charged feeling got stronger and stronger, as if it was reaching a tipping point. Celestine snarled and scratched the carpet as the snapping of the current in the air reached its peak.

And then I watched with wonder as, with one last push, the baby was born into the white towel Crowe was holding. The infant was smeared with vernix and fluid and blood, and had a purple scrunched-up face. Despite this, it was the single most beautiful thing I had ever seen.

"It's a girl!" Isadora shouted triumphantly, and I watched as the baby took its first shuddering breath, and Samantha took her last. The smoke fell to the floor like a damp towel, then dissipated.

The baby gave an almighty bawl, and I couldn't tear my eyes away from her. Crowe passed her to me and I wrapped her up in the receiving blanket. Usually I wouldn't want to hold a baby, never mind a newborn—knowing me, I'd drop the thing—but I didn't hesitate to take her from Crowe, who busied herself with clamping the cord and cutting it. I marveled at the child, light as a feather, who faded and shimmered in my arms. She stopped screaming and seemed to be searching my face with its swollen eyes. She didn't look dead, I thought, but then I felt her wrist for a heartbeat and there was none. Lou gestured at me to pass the baby to her. She took the bundle and laid it on Sam's chest, then wrapped the dead woman's arms around it. The baby started crying again, and, sensing her mother so close, began rooting for milk. I was worried the infant would wriggle too much, and fall to the floor, so I stepped forward to make her more secure, but Lou shot her arm out to stop me, and her eyes said: *Wait.*

The little girl cried louder, her squashed face maroon with the effort of it all, while her mother's corpse faced the ceiling, slack-jawed. The baby kicked and rocked, trying to reach the promise of the milk she could smell. She almost toppled off Sam's motionless chest, and I had to stop myself from reaching out again. The three of us stood there, staring, hearts-in-throats. The bundle cried and snuffled and rocked, and then she did finally kick hard enough to shift herself off Sam's chest, and began to roll. I gasped as the baby tumbled, terrified that she'd hit the floor. Samantha's eyes clicked open and she caught her daughter in the crook of her arm.

CHAPTER 32
MAD BAD WORLD

W e made Samantha a cup of tea using the kettle that had been mercifully spared by the kitchen plant, and then realized she wouldn't be able to drink it.

"It'll take a while to get used to it," said Lou, and Samantha nodded. "There are things you won't be able to do anymore, but your new abilities will make up for that."

"Where will I go, now?" Sam asked, her voice husky; strained from the earlier screaming. She was nursing the baby, who was calm.

"Stay here," said Crowe. "Rest. Take care of your girl."

"I don't know anything about this. I don't know what to do."

It was rather a double-whammy, I thought. New to motherhood and to the limbo land that is deadling territory. Not an easy thing to navigate when you've just, well, died.

"Your husband will come for you," Lou said, starting to fade away. "He'll guide you."

"When?" Sam asked.

"He'll appear to you once your transition is complete. That's when you'll be able to move between the veils."

Samantha gazed down at her daughter and I saw a tear roll down her cheek, which she wiped away with the heel of her hand.

Lou saluted us and vanished, leaving only the slightest hint of smoke in the air.

And remember, I heard her say. *I'm not your pizza delivery guy,* and I couldn't help smiling. I looked down at the mug in my hand, which was still hot. I gave it to Crowe.

"Thank you for your help," I said. "I honestly don't know what I would have done without you."

"You would have managed," said Crowe, and sipped the tea. "Always have, always will."

"I don't know about that," I said.

"Stop it," she said. "Humility doesn't suit you."

I gave her a half-smile, and she returned it.

"Don't worry," said the witch. "I'll stay here with them while you're away."

There was no point in asking how she knew I had to get out of there.

"Thank you," I said.

I PULLED on my trench coat and took out the portal key, which had become invaluable. I didn't know how I had ever managed without it. Only when I looked down at the key did I realize how much I was shaking. I had to calm down if I was going to pull this off.

"It's going to be okay," I said to myself, out loud. "It's going to be okay."

Gizmo squeaked as he climbed into his usual spot in my pocket. I wasn't sure if he was agreeing or not.

If I could only get Gizmo close enough to Darick to pick up his scent, the ferret would be able to lead me the rest of the way. But there were limited opportunities as Darick was spending most of his time in the transfer van, which was locked down with a complicated enchantment that made it bulletproof, magically-speaking. It was blocking off his magical energy from us, and hence the scent that Gizmo could follow. I had to get closer to him, but I had no way of finding him if I wasn't able to unlock Musubarin's laptop. What I needed was the Ember Isles Penitentiary collection schedule: the itinerary that showed me where the van would be stopping at what times. We had to get to one of those collection points or we'd never get to Darick, manacled and speeding toward his destruction, which was in the opposite direction of the Copperfield Institute. In my mind, the Hammerskins were already smashing down the doors there and helping themselves to the canteen fridges, wrecking everything—and anyone—in their way.

"Gizmo," I said. "Please take me to Eafaris and Pepin Belore."

He nodded and stroked his whiskers. I closed my eyes and relaxed into the spell, clutching the key and thinking of the twins.

"Ianua Sit," I said, and I felt my body falling away into the portal.

WHEN WE ARRIVED at the Copperfield Institute I cried out. It was a smoother than usual landing—my gateway magic was improving—but what lay before my eyes was traumatic. The gate was smashed open. Some trees were flattened, as if the orcs had arrived in army tanks. I peered into the guard hut outside—empty. Then I saw the motionless body a few meters away, under the shade of the purple-blossomed jacaranda tree. I ran up to him and exclaimed in anguish at what I saw. Rusty, the bronze-pelted werewolf, who had worked as the security guard at the Institute for decades, lay murdered. He had returned to his lupine form in death, a great gash in his fur showing sinews, dark crusted blood, and bone. I reached out and touched his chest, and my hand sprang away in an age-old revulsion of death. I took a breath and reached out again, checking for his pulse, but I knew that his heart had stopped long ago.

"Faex," I said, feeling tears sting my eyes. I remembered when I had been there a couple of days before and he had

leapt at me with a hug, smelling vaguely of damp fur and dog pellets. The hot tears weren't for my own pain, but for that of his family. Rusty had a litter of kids, and grandkids, which would hear tonight that their father or grandfather was gone. And why? Just so that some damn Neo-Nazi orcs could grab anything they wanted, no matter the cost to good people and good families. It made me so angry, standing there, between his ripped-open body and the demolished gate, that I felt the raw power of the Void pour into my body and light me up. I felt the sparks under my skin, ready to be released, and I had to take a moment to push it all down. It's hard to think clearly when you're zinging with magical energy. It was not the time for action and loud spells and show-off magic. I had to creep into the school grounds undetected, and get the kids as quickly and quietly as I could. Once they were safely delivered to Ferra, who was stowed away with the rest of her family in the *The Cog*'s generous-sized basement, a la *Fantastic Mister Fox*, I would find a way to rescue Darick. That would be the time for big magic. Now was not the time to fight. I turned to make my way into the Copperfield Institute grounds, and that's when I saw the Hammerskin standing sentinel, just beyond the entrance, between the felled trees. I didn't know how long he had been watching me, but he had a leer on his face as if he were a hungry hyena and I was a juicy lamb cutlet. I sighed and reached for my crossbow. So much for making a quiet entrance.

CHAPTER 33
A CADILLAC PACKED WITH DYNAMITE

The Hammerskin began walking towards me, and he lifted his weapon: a baseball bat spiked with bent steel nails. I looked at the crossbow in my hands and wondered if the orc was worth an arrow, and decided that he was not. I had a long day ahead of me and limited ammunition.

I had so much magic fizzing in my fingers that, despite my initial reservations, it would make more sense to send a bolt of magic his way than a bolt of smooth tempered steel. I swapped my bow for my silver wand, which was already warm and humming with potential energy, and I pointed it at the vile creature who was watching me with his cadmium eyes.

"Volas!" I shouted, and whipped the tip of my wand up to the sky, as if I was salmon-fishing in Yemen rather than disarming a particularly vicious-looking orc. The nail bat flew out of his bratwurst-fingered hands and into the air above. He frowned and blinked at his empty mitt, and didn't

even see the Grim Reaper standing behind him, chuckling and rubbing his palms, courtesy of a particularly wily girl wizard.

"Contendis!" I yelled, and the bat came straight back down, whacking him on the head with the business end. It wasn't pretty, but it was satisfying. His sweat-shiny skull came apart like a watermelon at a shooting range. His knees gave way, and he fell with a wet thud onto the hard driveway tarmac, splattering it with brain matter and blood.

I was glad he was dead, and I was glad it was I who had killed him, but I did not delight in the violence.

Ashing a vampire is one thing, but tearing into a man's skull is the kind of memory that you can't uncarve. I wanted to put as much distance as possible between myself and the orc, but as I walked past him I realized I'd be silly to leave the blinged-out bat there just because it was gory-looking, so I went up to him and wrenched it free from his shattered skull bone. It came away with a sickening crunch that made me cringe, but when I held the weapon in my hands it made me feel fortified.

I walked along the extensive driveway, not paying too much attention to the destroyed trees and broken beer bottles because they made me feel a deep ache of regret.

Was it the end of the Copperfield Institute? If the Hammerskins had already annexed the place, would the twins still be here? Where was Directress Copperfield?

As soon as I reached the buildings I slunk between them, creeping in the shadows for cover. I scuttled closer to the hostel and could hear a cacophony of brutes' voices laughing, and chinking glasses. It should have sent a chill down my spine, but instead I was cheered by it. These Hammerskins weren't organized soldiers, they were savages just along for the ride. They were not chatting strategy or figuring out the best way to overthrow the Council. They were just there to rob and kill and pillage. It was a political joyride in a Cadillac packed with dynamite, with a fuse they didn't even know was burning.

The same flame lit a spark of hope in my heart. Maybe, just maybe, we could win this war. With enough smarts and bravery we might be able to defeat the barbarians in our midst.

When I reached the first quad, I saw that the copper statue of Minerva had been knocked over, and she was lying face-down in the grass. That hope-flame flickered, and almost went out.

"Jax!" came a hard whisper. I froze, and looked around. "Jax!"

It was Eafaris Belore's voice. He sounded close, almost close enough to touch. I stepped back, confused.

"Eafy?" I whispered back. I looked and looked, but I couldn't see him. "Eafy?"

Then there was a shimmer in the air, and the boy appeared. Then the shimmer beside him turned into Pepin. We hugged each other hard and pressed our cheeks together. I was so relieved to see them. I heard other children's voices but they didn't show themselves. Perhaps they found my nail bat disconcerting.

"What happened?" I asked. What I really meant was, *How are you still here, alive and unharmed?*

Pepin pulled a bottle of bright saffron-colored liquid from her school blazer pocket. "Directress Copperfield got into the potions lab before they arrived. She and Sir Sparks made enough *Invisibilis Factus* for all the orphans."

Pepin's use of the word "orphans" was a jab in the heart. I wanted to pull them tightly to me again and tell them they were not orphans, that they are loved, fiercely and deeply. But, of course, that didn't change the fact that their parents were dead. I knew that, and the knowledge stung.

"The directress refused to leave the school grounds, so she found a way to stay. She put an enchantment on her house so the Hammerskins couldn't get in—"

"—She couldn't do it over the whole school but at least we have the house."

"So that's where we're staying, but since we're invisible we like to hang out around here."

Sometimes talking to the Belore twins was like watching a tennis match. They spoke as if they were one person, or an old couple, finishing each other's sentences.

"We try to get close to them," said Pepin.

"To the orcs," said Eafaris.

"No," I said. "You mustn't. It's dangerous. You must tell the others to stay at the house. It's safer."

"But it's more fun out here," said Pepin. "We get to eavesdrop on the Hammerskins and then we tell Sir Sparks what they're planning."

"Usually they're pretty dumb plans," said Eafaris, "but every now and then we hear something important."

"We're spies," said Pepin, her eyes bright. "We're gathering intel."

"Well," I said. I knew I shouldn't be encouraging them, but it was pretty handy having a fleet of invisible children listening in on the Hammerskin discussions.

"They're not very clever," said Eafaris. "They drove an army tank in here and then drove over a giant rock to show off."

"Bye-bye army tank," said Pepin.

"So much for intelligence," said Eafy, and he smiled. It was the first time I had seen a genuine smile on his face since his father went missing.

Pepin also smiled. "We play tricks on them," she said, and giggled.

My anxiety spiked. I didn't want to know what would happen if the savages got hold of one of the children. "What do you mean?"

"We practice our magic on them."

"You mustn't," I said. "It's too dangerous."

"They have their plans to take over the Realm, but we have one of our own."

"And what's that?" I asked.

"If we keep causing trouble here, they'll think the place is haunted, and leave us alone."

I laughed out loud. "That's a good plan," I said, ruffling Eafy's hair.

"Abel Bishop turned all the milk sour this morning, just as the orcs were tucking into their cereal. And he kept on making the toast pop out of the toaster, and they'd all jump."

"Zanele keeps opening all the cabinet doors. And turning on the fans."

"Xolisa put a rather complicated spell on the toilets that makes them flush as soon as anyone sits down on them."

"Robyn magicked the canteen's butcher knives so that they follow the Hammerskins around, just floating in the air behind them. One of the orcs only noticed it when he had finished showering and then when he opened the shower curtain and saw it he screamed like a little girl," said Eafaris.

Pepin punched him on the arm.

"You two are coming with me. You need to be somewhere safer."

"Aw," said Pepin.

"I know," I said. "Look, I can see how much fun it must be to torment Neo-Nazi orcs, but that potion will run out soon," I looked pointedly at the bottle in Pepin's hand. "And the Directress won't be able to keep that protection spell on her house forever. Those take a lot of magic. Then what will you do?"

They looked at each other with wide eyes.

"Besides," I said. "Ferra wants you to be with her."

The disappointment disappeared and they looked cheerful again. Ferra was their dwarf fairy godmother just as she was mine. I guessed they'd rather be with her than anywhere else in the world. We huddled in the middle of the quad, next to the felled statue of Minerva and her elusive owl, and we all held onto the portal key while I uttered the gateway spell and hoped for a soft landing.

CHAPTER 34
PEPPY PENTESTER

"Oof!" exclaimed Eafy as we hit the hard floor of *The Copper Cog*'s basement.

Pepin rubbed her shin and looked at me. "You need to practice your magic."

"Story of my life," I said.

Ferra's voice boomed. "Who do we have here?"

The twins ran into her arms. The basement was warm and lit by golden lanterns, and the air smelled like spices, toasted coconut, and sugar. There was even one of the copper clocks ticking cheerfully on the wall.

"You'll be pleased to know that Fig whipped up a makeshift oven for me," said Ferra, glowing. "So we won't run out of roasts or cakes. And it doubles as a heater."

She stepped aside to show us the "makeshift oven." It was a thing of beauty. Now, I know I'm hardly handy in the kitchen —I'm convinced that my pots and pans at home live in abject fear of me reaching for one of them—but this oven made even me want to cook something. It was a steampunk work of art, all copper and steel pipes and dials. And it was, at that very moment, baking some delicious smelling rusks.

"That's beautiful," I said. Without looking up, Fig grunted.

"He makes fun of me, you know he does, about being a doomsday prepper," said Ferra. "But do you remember that day he was making something out in the restaurant? Banging away like that when you and I went into the lab for your new crossbow?"

"I remember," I said. It was the same day Ferra had volunteered to foster the Belore twins.

"This oven is what he was making," Ferra said. "*Happy wife, happy life,*" she had said that day.

The children were all busy with various crafts, creating the things that would make their stay easier to bear, from knitting blankets and socks to painting art for the walls. One of the dwarf children was weaving a basket, another drawing a technical drawing on how he was planning on extracting drinking water from the pipes that ran in the compacted soil above their ceiling. There was also a blueprint for a boring device, and a technical article written by Elon Musk.

"Looks like you're doing well down here," I said. We shared a glance that acknowledged the Fernaks' heartbreak of losing the pub and their house, but it was shot through with the silver lining that they were all still alive, and together.

"You know what they say. Home is where the magical steam-punk oven is," I said. It was corny, but I was trying to keep the atmosphere light.

"Thank you, Jinx," Ferra said. "Thank you for bringing the twins home."

I winked at Eafaris and Pepin, and they winked back. "Thank you, Jax," they said in chorus.

I was about to leave when I realized I didn't have a destination to portal to, because I hadn't been able to decode Musubarin's password on his laptop.

"Do you by any chance know anything about hacking into someone's computer?" I asked Ferra.

"Nope," she said, "but I'm sure we could work something out."

Unfortunately, I didn't have time to spend doing that. I wished for Chuck Winnow at that moment. He owed me one, after all.

"Hacking?" said Eafy, looking up from helping a younger dwarf with her wood carving. "Pepin can do that."

Pepin looked at me with big eyes and nodded.

"She's top of the class in computers," he said. "Volt calls her Peppy Pentester. She said she's going to be the next Bill Gateway."

"Who? What? You're making me feel old."

"Madame Voltaire is our computer teacher. We call her Volt for short. Pip's her favorite. Just tell her what you need her to do."

"I need the Ember Isles convict transfer schedule," I said. "The transfer van that left last night had Darick on it."

Both twins looked at me with wide eyes, and I could swear I heard Ferra gulp. I unzipped the backpack and brought out Musubarin's machine.

"I can't get past the password," I said. "I tried a few options and got locked out."

Pepin took the computer from me and sat down on a beanbag against the wall. She put the machine on her lap and began typing.

"You got locked out because you were trying to go through the front door," she said, frowning at the screen.

While we waited for her, Eafaris pulled me aside. "We're safe now, thanks to you," he said.

"You seemed to be doing pretty well at Copperfield on your own." I smiled, but he didn't return it. His eyes were sincere, and focused, and I could feel the magic coming off him in gentle waves. They reminded me of how powerful, and accurate, the twins' combined magic had been in the volcano pocket realm. They had held hands and finished Deadwing off with the notorious death spell that even I was afraid to use.

"You're going to get Darick?" he asked. "That seems a very dangerous thing to do."

"I'll try my best to stay alive," I said. "I want to be around long enough to have some of those rusks Ferra is baking."

Eafaris still didn't smile. Tough crowd.

"I want to give you something," he said. His hands traveled up to his neck, unclasped his gold chain, and put it in my palm. It was his father's Dragon's Eye amulet. It shone in the golden light of the lanterns on the wall.

"Oh," I said. "I can't."

"Dad's amulet, Mom's necklace. They'll help you. Help you focus your power."

It was the only thing the twins had of their parents down there. I knew how much those kinds of things meant on cold, lonely nights.

"I can't," I said.

"You have to," he said, and suddenly it snaked around my neck and fastened itself. Before I could say anything else, Pepin piped up.

"Found it!" she said. "I've taken a screenshot and sent it to your phone."

Just then my phone beeped in my pocket. She looked pleased, but then her face fell. It looked eerie in the blue light of the screen.

"What's wrong?" I asked, pulling out my phone.

"We've got a problem," she said, and I just blinked at her.

The Void knows I did not need another "problem." I looked down at my phone and opened the screenshot.

"Filius Canis," I said.

One of the toddler dwarfs looked up from his needlepoint. "What does that mean?" he asked.

"It means *son of a b—*" said the older one, next to him, who didn't finish his sentence because Ferra shot him a look that would have made a goblin glass dagger look blunt.

I looked at my phone, then at the clock on the wall. It was six minutes past two.

The last stop before the transfer van hit the coastline would be at a place called the Crystal Clink, and they were scheduled to pick that prisoner up at 2:15 p.m.

"Oh, boy," I said. Portaling there would take a few minutes, but it was still cutting it really fine. It was my last chance to save him. As far as I knew, they drove the transfer van directly onto the Ember Isles ferry, so I had to reach him before they got there. I suddenly felt frozen by the hopelessness of the situation, but Ferra grabbed my hand and shook me out of it.

"You can make it," she said. "Don't waste another moment."

Pepin put something in my hand. I looked down to see that it was her bottle of invisibility potion. *Thank you,* I mouthed, putting it in my pocket.

My breath was shaky when I brought out the key and asked Gizmo for help. I almost stuttered when I cast the gateway spell, which may have been a disaster, and that made my heart beat even faster. I didn't have time to wave to the twins or the Fernaks before I was whipped into the gray tunnel, forgetting again to ask for a soft landing, something I regretted profoundly when I landed face-first on a hot strip of concrete, smashing my hip and breaking my nose in the process. It sent an explosion of stars into my brain, blinding me. I had to spend a minute lying there, trying to clear my head. Just as I was about to get up I felt someone's heel grind into my shoulder. I heard a gun being cocked. My hip bone was humming with pain, and bright red blood cascaded from my nose.

"Now you stay right there, wizard," said an unfamiliar voice. Then he spoke into his walkie talkie. "Just as expected," he drawled. "Ms. Jacquelyn Denna Knight."

CHAPTER 35

EYES THE COLOR OF ICE

I groaned and tried to shake the silver static from my head as the blood kept streaming from my nose. I didn't understand what was going on. The shoulder-grinding army boot flipped me over onto my back, and the sun seemed a hundred shades too bright. The man was a silhouette with a rifle. I tried to shield my eyes from the glare and he jammed the gun into my chest.

"I didn't tell you you could move," he growled, pinning me down with the barrel.

They had been expecting me, I thought. *They knew I was coming.*

I squinted and looked around at where we were. I saw a slice of bright blue sky, and not a lot else. But then he shifted his weight on to his other foot, and I was able to see his black military uniform and badge. Onyx Security. The company that facilitated the Ember Isles transfers.

"Looking for your boyfriend?" he sneered. "He's not here. He boarded the ferry at two o'clock."

"You're lying," I said.

He chuckled and pushed the gun further into my chest, setting off a new wave of pain.

"You can't keep me here against my will," I said.

"Oh yes I can. In fact I have strict instructions to detain you."

"I haven't done anything wrong."

"Huh," he said. "That's not what I heard. I heard you have a list of offenses as long as a fae's tale."

The conversation felt like it was a shallow-sleep dream. Really all I could hear was the man's voice saying over and over that Darick had boarded the ferry at 2 o'clock.

Darick was gone, and I didn't know if I wanted to live without him. My future looked bleached of love or hope. I didn't want to live in a world where the Scorpion squad was run by a menace like Musubarin, or the Realm destroyed by thuggish Hammerskins who didn't think twice about stealing family homes or killing good werewolves like Rusty. But still, that flame in my heart was alive. That small fire kept burning, kept telling me that I needed to keep going. For Nilve SaltySnap. For the Fernaks and the twins. For Darick. For Gizmo. For the memory of my parents, which made my silver wand vibrate against my injured pelvis.

Just then I noticed that my nose had stopped bleeding and my vision had cleared. I frowned at a point in the distance and said, "Who's that?"

The man had guessed at my cheap tricks, so he didn't take his eyes off me. I had expected that. What he hadn't guessed at was my ability to create chimeras off the top of my head and without moving my lips. The picture of the slaughtered Rusty loomed in my mind. The point in the distance, which was, before, an empty space, became a loping wolf with a growling smile and a pelt the color of corroded iron. I thought it held some kind of poetic justice.

The wolf was silent as it approached, and despite my position—prostrate, aching, skin burning on the sun-baked concrete beneath me—I still admired its elegant stealth and its eyes the color of ice. I marveled, not for the first time, how incredible our brains are, being able to create such beautiful creatures from nothing. It was a figment of my imagination, but my magic brought it to life.

Attack.

The wolf leapt at the Onyx man. He fell, dropping his rifle, which clattered down beside me. He shouted for the wolf to leave him alone and tried to roll away from the creature's snapping jaws. I jumped up and grabbed the gun, confirmed the safety switch was off, then pointed its long barrel at the shrieking guard.

"Heel!" I said to the wolf. It looked up at me, then came to sit at my feet. I had never been able to make a chimera listen to my directions before, so when the wolf obeyed me it stoked my confidence. I felt powerful for a moment, rifle in hand, wolf at my heel.

I reached for one of the pairs of handcuffs in my trench coat pocket and threw them at the Onyx man.

"Cuff yourself," I said. I liked the way it sounded like an insult. Sometimes my sense of humor was immature, and I was okay with that.

His gaze didn't waver. He clicked the cuffs on, then showed me they were secured.

"Take me to your desk," I said. He hesitated. The wolf growled, showing his magnificent canines. The man closed his eyes for a moment then turned and began to walk, head bowed, spirit broken. I can imagine what he was thinking. He'd have to find a job somewhere else, now. Perhaps as a shoplifter-spotter at Pick-n-Pay supermarket, or a bag-searcher at goblin punk rock concerts. Even if he wasn't fired —which he certainly would be—he'd have to endure the mocking that would accompany the legacy of having been defeated by a *girl wizard* and her make-believe pet.

HE LED us to his hole in the wall, a cramped office with a stained and scratched desk and a cup of coffee long cold, with the milk skin on its surface to prove it. The bashed-up thermos flask stood, reproachfully, in the corner.

I was surprised at the color of the coffee. I would have guessed this guy would drink his black. Then I heard the toilet flush and the restroom door unlock, and I aimed the rifle at the stranger on the other side of it, who I guessed was the owner of the milky coffee. She opened the door and looked straight into the barrel of my borrowed rifle, and put up her hands. She didn't say a word. I reached into my pocket and pulled out the second pair of handcuffs. What were the chances of needing both of them that day? Who knew. All I knew was that I wasn't going to take that kind of luck for granted. I threw them at her and repeated my new favorite insult.

"Cuff yourself." Before she clicked the second bracelet closed I looped it under the chain of the man's handcuffs, so they were locked together. Then I took the bicycle chain I had seen outside and attached them both to the burglar bars of the small side window and reset the code to the numerical equivalent of JINX.

"You can't leave us like this," the man said. I turned the rifle on him. The wolf—who I must admit I was growing attached to—growled again, showing his wet black lips and fantastic fangs.

I STILL HAD the rifle pointed at the woman's chest. "How did you know I was coming?"

She was about to talk when the man told her to keep quiet.

"The wolf hasn't eaten," I said, and the man decided to stop talking, which I thought was a good decision.

"I'm not going to ask you again," I said to the woman, pretending to apply pressure to the trigger.

She shook her head and bit her lips in a nervous gesture. "An alert came through," she said, and gestured at the radio system on the desk. "Said you'd be here at around two p.m. Armed and dangerous. They said to keep you here."

My own stupidity rose up and slapped me across the face. I had fallen for another trap. Musubarin had remotely planted that fake transfer schedule on his laptop, and I had taken the bait.

Deodamnatus! I wanted to kick myself, but had to act cool. Bloody Musubarin had tricked me into going to the *Laser Dungeon,* and because I hadn't figured it out in time, I had fallen for this ruse, too. I was glad that I had broken his nose. My hand flew up to feel the state of mine. A nose for a nose.

"I asked for some kind of warrant," she said. "Some kind of formal instruction, but they said there wasn't time for that."

"That sounds like Musubarin's style," I said.

"Musubarin?" she said. "The command didn't come from Musubarin."

"What?" I felt like I had just stuck a wet finger into a plug point.

"Usually I'd presume innocence," she said. "Didn't understand why a civilian with a clean-ish record would all of a sudden become *armed and dangerous.*"

I just looked at her, trying to understand.

"Or, if you did become dangerous, I figured maybe you had a reason."

We shared a look of understanding; of past trauma. Despite

her badge, she had more in common with me than the fool she was chained to.

I looked at the cheap clock on the wall. 2:24.

"Did the ferry really leave at 2 o'clock?" I asked.

The man glared at her, but she ignored him. "The van boards the ferry at two," she said. "But the ferry departs at half-past."

Slight relief, and then more panic. Darick was already secured on the ferry, and I had less than six minutes to find a way to get to him. I slung the gun over my shoulder, and they both sagged with relief. I collected their mobile phones and walkie-talkies, and put them on top of the radio system, then I pointed my wand at the pile of tech and yelled *"Fiat fulgar!"*

A bright blue current bolted out of my wand and slammed into the machine, short-circuiting it, and frying the phones. There was a soft *pop* from the transmission box, the blinking lights flickered and dimmed, and a plume of gray smoke went up in the air. I saw an Ember Isles Port pass on a red lanyard lying on the desk. I grabbed it and put it around my neck.

The man was about to say something again, but the wolf took a step toward him so the words died on his lips. I threw the keys for the woman's handcuffs at her, and she caught them in a practiced movement.

Thank you, her eyes said, and I blinked in return. The wolf stayed to watch them.

CHAPTER 36
INVISIBILIS FACTUS

I chanted the gateway spell while I clutched the portal key, The Ember Isles Port pass, and Gizmo's little paw. It was a complicated destination, but we got there in less than a minute. Happily for my bruised hipbone and probably-broken nose, the landing was uncharacteristically soft, and cushioned by soft gold-green grasses.

Despite its macabre reputation, the coastline and scenery at the port was beautiful. Stark blue sky reflected vividly by the ocean, waves crashing over and over again, hurling themselves against the rough black rocks. Gulls wheeling and squalling overhead, and the taste of salt in the warm air. I could see the ferry from where I stood, and the transfer van parked neatly in its prescribed bay. There were a few Onyx officials striding about, wearing the same uniform and badges as the two guards I had just left at the Crystal Clink depot. The whole area was fenced off with black barbed wire and yellow *Prohibited Entry* signs. They were detaching the boat from its moorings, ready to sail.

My blood was rushing in my ears as I tried to think of a strategy. In my experience, adrenaline blasting into your bloodstream is never a good way to get a solid plan under your belt. Still, I tried.

If I could just get into that van without being spotted, I was sure I'd find a way to set Darick free. The problem was that I needed to break that security enchantment. I had no idea how to do it, and no time to figure it out.

Breathe, I reminded myself. *Breathe.*

I let Gizmo out of my pocket, and took out the half-drunk bottle of *Invisibilis Factus* potion that Pepin had slipped into my hand as I had left the Fernak fox den. I pulled the cork out and had a large sip of the tincture, which was the same bright orange color as the pincushion flowers that surrounded me. I didn't have to wait long for it to work. Soon the tips of my fingers were shimmering. They turned to mirror and then to glass, and then they disappeared altogether. My hands vanished next, then the rest of my body, as if the air was eating me. I felt a barrage of hailstones inside my body, hard and cold, and when I looked down again, I was totally invisible. All I could see were the bright flowers swaying in the breeze.

I scrabbled down the hill, my hip flaring with pain at every step. I ran down onto the paved surface of the pedestrian pathway, and then down to the actual port, which was oil-stained and dirty from the traffic it endured. Waves lapped against its sturdy structure. There were three officers walking about, administering last-minute checks. I moved past them as quietly as I could, although my own breathing sounded loud in my ears. I thanked the Void for the white noise of the ocean as I approached the van and put my palms on it, trying to get a feel for which brand of magic was locking it down. I was concentrating hard, so when the whistle sounded to begin the journey I jumped about a mile high. One of the officers frowned in my direction, so I stood still and practiced not breathing until he looked away.

Problem number one: The officers were all armed and alert. They looked like the kind of people who shot first and asked questions later.

Problem number two: I didn't know how to unlock the magic of the van.

Problem number three: If I was able to open the vehicle, all the other dangerous criminals would be able to escape, too.

Problem number four: The ferry was leaving. I was heading to the Ember Isles.

CHAPTER 37
A POPSICLE IN UNIFORM

The whistle sounded again, and one of the officers called out. Time to sail.

Every fiber of my being wanted to get off that ferry. I put my palms on the cool steel of the transfer van, and I finally got a glimpse of the enchantment that had been used to keep the vehicle secure. It was, from what I could tell, an advanced protection spell. Usually it would take me a couple of hours to work out the various layers of magic, but I had less than a minute. The adrenaline had already spiked my power, and the pain of my injured hip and smashed nose augmented it further. The magic coursed through me in a clean blue torrent, so powerful it took my breath away. With clutching fingers I found the twins' Dragon's Eye amulet that was hanging around my neck and I remembered their loss and grief, which so closely mirrored my own. These emotions blustering through me magnified my magic like I had never experienced before, and what had seemed so impossible a minute earlier suddenly seemed easy.

Break the protection spell, get Darick, vámanos. *Right?*

Break. Destroy. Rumpis.

But then the ferry's engine started up, and we started moving, gliding slowly on the salty sea. I squeezed the amulet tighter and scrunched up my eyes.

Rumpis! I thought, as loudly and clearly as I could.

I drove the power from my body in an intense outburst of magic that flew over the van, snapping the protection spell like the wishbone of an unlucky chicken.

"Hey!" yelled one of the officers, reaching for his gun. "Freeze!"

Still reeling from the magnitude of the spell, I felt confused for an instant. The spell had caused a loud crackle in the air, alerting the men to the van, but why did the officer say *"Freeze?"*

I looked down at my boots, and saw that they, along with my legs, were very much visible. My intense magic had broken the security enchantment of the van, but it had destroyed the *Invisibilis Factus* spell, too.

Not ready to launch more magic of that magnitude, and not wanting to kill the officer, I chose my wand over the rifle on my shoulder. I shot my arm out at him before he had time to fire.

"Glaciem Exquiris!" I yelled, and a thin streak of ice-blue magic froze him to the spot, stiffening his arms and slowing his heart. His frozen face looked at me, agape. I heard

another gun clicking behind me, and I spun around, wand in hand, and slung the same spell at the other officer. *"Glaciem Exquiris!"* I shouted, and I turned the man into ice: a popsicle in a uniform. I couldn't spot the third man, so I turned back to the van and clasped the Dragon's Eye amulet again. It was in my left hand, and my wand in my right.

"Ignem Exquiris!" I said. The wand became a blowtorch with a fierce cyan-pink flame, and I used it to score through the huge lock on the back door. The amulet was warm in my hand and it felt like it was speaking to me, telling me I was doing well. We were a couple of meters of lapping water away from the quayside. Just too far to jump, even if your parkour skills were on fleek. The lock gave way, and I wrenched the heavy door open.

Six pairs of eyes blinked back at me.

"Jax!" shouted Darick. He looked deathly pale: shocked and anxious, but when I melted his manacles and he was able to stand and rub his wrists, a hint of color returned to his cheeks. Disorientated, he stumbled toward me. The other prisoners started moaning and begging.

"Free me!"

"Hey! What about me?"

"I'm innocent!"

I saw a face I recognized, then two. Ophelia and Dylan Knox. "Help us!" they cried. But then the picture of Hettie Frost flashed in on me, the image of her fingertips rubbed down to the bone. I also couldn't help thinking of the half-knitted sailboat jersey in Woolfmoon's house, while she lay under the clear bathwater, staring up at the ceiling. A grandson who would never feel the affection of his grandmother again.

I ignored their pleas.

"Let's go!" I said to Darick, and he climbed out of the van. I turned my back, and a vaguely familiar voice said quietly: "It's you."

I spun around to see who had said it, and saw the werewolf who had helped me at the EverShade night market. Without thinking it through, I melted his restraints, and he jumped out of the vehicle and joined us. We were thirty meters or so now from dry land, and the motion of the boat and smell of the petrol was making me feel seasick.

Suddenly the third officer appeared and took aim at us. He pulled the trigger of his revolver and it sounded like a lightning crack. The bullet hit me in the chest. The power of it knocked me backwards, to the ground, and sending a new current of pain to my hip. He turned the gun on Darick, who seemed unsteady on his feet, blinking in the sunlight he was no longer used to. Still on the ground, my breath knocked out of my burning lungs, I looked down at my chest, expecting the worst. My coat had stopped the missile from penetrating my skin, but that didn't stop it from hurting like a *filius canis*.

"Darick!" I shouted, as I heard the bang of another bullet leaving the chamber. It was as if time stood still, then, as I saw the bullet traveling in the air toward him. Also in slow-motion, the werewolf shifted into his lupine form and leapt at Darick, knocking him to the ground just in time to dodge the bullet.

"Impedio!" I shouted at the officer. His finger froze on the trigger, then the rest of his limbs followed suit.

I hauled air into my lungs and stood up, rubbing my breast-bone where the bullet had struck me. I looked at the port, which was then around half a kilometer away. We looked at each other, then all took a running jump and dived into the opalescent ocean.

The sensation of the sparkling water was at first refreshing after all the heated magic and adrenaline and dizzying petrol fumes on the ferry, but soon the cold began to leech my energy. I found my swimming rhythm, cutting the water with my arms and churning it white behind me as the cold sucked at my lungs and sang in my bones.

After around twenty minutes my muscles began to show fatigue, and my fingers were numb, but I kept my head down and continued swimming, making sure that Darick and the werewolf were keeping pace. Towards the end I was gasping and trying not to choke on the water. I urgently needed to rest, and worried that I wouldn't make the last hundred meters. I was wondering if any of the spells in my arsenal could somehow help us, but worried that I wouldn't be able to cast it without swallowing water and/or sinking. It got more and more difficult to keep afloat, and my arms stopped obeying my strict instructions to keep going. I imagined a White shark just below the surface, razor teeth flashing in the dappled water as he watched my limbs flailing against the expanse of deep blue water, ready to attack. The thought motivated me to keep kicking. We were almost there.

I looked up at the wharf, hoping the sight of it being nearby would give me the final push I needed to get there. I saw the emergency lights flashing, and heard the siren wailing. A troop of men in black uniforms stood on the embankment, their automatic rifles trained on us.

I PANICKED and misjudged the level of the choppy water, taking in a huge lungful of it. I began to cough and splutter, and was finding it difficult to keep my head above the water as I choked. Darick saw me struggling and began swimming smoothly in my direction. I couldn't catch a breath, and my exhausted, oxygen-deprived muscles began to fail. Darick was a few meters away when I knew for sure I was going to sink. Then all of a sudden there was a hailstorm of bullets in the water around us, and he cried out and disappeared beneath the water.

Darick! I tried to shout, *Darick!* but there was no air to float my words, and it stayed a gargle in my lungs. I looked around for the werewolf, but he was also gone. The lack of oxygen began to steal my vision. A fresh storm of bullets boiled the ocean around me. I felt one missile bite into my thigh, and another cracked my collarbone. I thought of how the White shark would follow the scent of my blood; a trailing ribbon of red underwater smoke.

I became very cold, and confused, as if my organs were shutting down. My mind felt as storm-tossed as the water I was flailing in. I stopped fighting. Stopped trying to force my heart to keep beating when Fate had made it very clear that my time was up. I gave in to my worn out body, relinquishing myself to the ocean that seemed so intent on swallowing me up. That's when I felt the heavy jaws clamping down on my legs.

Shark, I thought. *That didn't take you very long.* And my body was yanked under the hungry dark water.

CHAPTER 38
A BEAUTIFUL DREAM

Death was like a beautiful dream. It embraced me without restraint.

I stopped panicking, my heart rested, my body was cool and weightless. The water that surrounded me pressed in on my skin, flowing over and around me, swirling my body in its gentle currents while the sun sparkled on the surface above. When Darick appeared I wasn't surprised. It felt like it was meant to be. Darick and I would die together, dancing in each other's arms. He reached out to me, and I to him, and he pulled me through the water toward him, and hugged me tight. His lips found mine as we floated down and I thought, *this is right. This is how it was supposed to end.* My black trench coat flared out around my legs like the skirt of a ballgown, and I relaxed even further. I was a dying rose. I gave myself up to him, going limp in his arms in a pose of total surrender.

But then instead of the long-awaited kiss I was expecting, he blew a violent gust of air into my mouth, and I started choking again. I coughed and spluttered, and my legs started kicking without my directing them to do so. Darick blew again, forcing oxygen into my sleeping lungs, and I turned on my side and heaved a bucketful of water out of my mouth. There was rough ground beneath my wrecked body, and the air was cool on my skin. I was out of the water—*how?*—and when I opened my eyes just a crack I saw Darick kneeling beside me. I realized he had been giving me mouth-to-mouth resuscitation. Judging by my bruised breastbone, I guessed he had done some chest compressions, too.

He grabbed my chin with one hand—fear making his touch rougher than usual—and clicked his fingers with the other hand.

"Can you hear me?" he demanded. Listening to his voice broke something inside me. I started to cry. He swept me up in his arms right there on the hard sea cave floor, our sodden clothes squelching together, and clutched my shivering, spluttering body to his. I wept into his wet chest and put his knuckles to my cheek, and wept some more. The closeness of his body, and his soothing nonsense melted-honey words broke me down further, until I was nothing. Until I was a wisp, and then the same words built me back up again, and I finally stopped trembling.

"Your heart stopped," he told me, as if I didn't already know.

I looked into his eyes.

How many times would this man bring me back from the brink of death?

I saw the werewolf loping around the cave, pacing, frowning. Even in his human form he scented the air with damp fur, reminding me of Rusty. He looked at me, his eyes lupine-bright despite the dim light.

"How will we get out of here?" he asked. He was restless and needed to move his body. The cave was too small for his animal spirit, and it was clear that there was no way out.

"I can portal us," I said, reaching into my pocket and bringing out the skeleton key. Both men's faces showed instant relief. Feeling the empty pocket made me worry about Gizmo.

Darick helped me up, and in that movement I smelled the crimson on him.

"You're hurt?" I asked, remembering the bullets churning up the surface of the sea just before he had clamped my legs and pulled me under.

He shrugged it off. "It's nothing."

"You've been shot," I said. "I can smell it. The gunpowder and the blood."

"Superficial," he said. "Already mostly healed."

I felt my nose, and then my hip. Neither seemed damaged anymore.

"Thank you," I said, and Darick touched my cheek.

"We'll portal back to my flat," I said. "Everywhere else is too dangerous."

They both nodded.

"But I have a stop to make, first."

I offered them both a sip of the invisibility potion, and then we all held onto the key as I cast the spell that would deposit us back at the golden grasses of the hill above the harbour. A dozen Onyx officers in black uniforms were combing the land and the sea for our bodies.

"Why are we back here?" growled the fresh air next to me, who I guessed was the werewolf. I knew I was taking a risk. An officer began walking in our direction, gun clasped in both hands as he swept left and right.

Come on, I thought. *Come on!* But I didn't have to wait long. Within a minute, Gizmo came running towards me and leapt into my arms, despite my being invisible. He snuggled down into his usual pocket, disappearing under the spell as he did so. It couldn't have been very pleasant, the coat being thoroughly soaked. We all held the key again and I was about to cast the gateway spell when Darick exclaimed, which made the nearby officer look directly at us. We were still concealed, so he just frowned and blinked and increased his pace. I started the gateway spell again, under my breath, but Darick grabbed my forearm, making me jump.

"Look," he said, a hard whisper next to my ear, and I looked at the ferry in the distance. I was in a hurry to get out of there. The officer was way too close for comfort, and his trigger finger was itchy. I could tell by the way it danced on the metal. I was cold and wet and nervous as hell, and I wanted to go, but Darick was telling me to watch the boat with the prisoners on it. I looked at it again, thinking of the Knoxes and the other bleak faces I had seen chained inside the van, and at that moment there was an ear-splitting explosion. The ferry exploded with a giant roar of flame and smoke, as if that van had been packed with nitroglyceride instead of human convicts. The officer who had been stalking us in the grass turned and looked at the ocean as the pieces of flaming debris rained down into the blue sea. He dropped his gun and put his hands to his head, watching the fire burn and send black smoke into the air. Then he seemed to pull himself together and pick up his revolver again. He forgot about whatever he had heard on the hill and ran down to join his team on the quay below.

My stomach felt leaden, thinking about the implications of the blast. Musubarin had never wanted Darick to reach the Ember Isles. He had wanted him dead.

"Ianua Sit," I whispered, and we all grabbed onto the key, and the gateway spell took like a spark on a piece of dry kindling. It whisked us out of the air of salt and smoke and deposited us roughly and unceremoniously on the cheap balding carpet of my haunted apartment.

We stayed on the floor for a moment to regain our bearings and watch our fingers turn from shimmer, to glass, to flesh.

"Smooth," growled the werewolf, rubbing his elbow.

"You're welcome," I said.

Crowe appeared, holding Celestine, who looked regal in his navy coat. "You took your time."

I looked up at her. "The Knoxes are dead," I said.

She didn't flinch. "Good. Cup of tea?"

CHAPTER 39
CONGRATS ON THE COCKTAIL PICKLE

"I need to go," said Darick.

My heart lurched. "No! I've only just got you back."

"It's wild country out there," said Crowe, looking pointedly at the window.

"Jo'burg has always been wild country," said the werewolf. I guess if anyone should know, it would be him.

I was desperate for Darick to stay. Was it so much to ask? Just a couple of hours' downtime after everything we'd been through? I wanted to just lie in his arms. I needed his skin next to mine. Most importantly, I needed him to be safe. Having him in a dangerous situation made me feel intensely vulnerable.

Darick took my hands and looked into my eyes. "I'll be back soon. There's something I need to sort out."

I had a feeling it had something to do with the fact that he had just escaped the ferry explosion that was meant to take his life.

"Stay here," I said, hating the tears that welled up in my eyes. "Stay here where it's safe."

"Nowhere is safe," he said.

He hugged me, hard, then kissed my still-salty cheek and squeezed my waist. He said goodbye.

AFTER HE LEFT, I felt absolutely bereft.

"Cheer up, wizard," said Izzy. "He'll be back."

I hung my coat up, walked to my bedroom, and kicked off my boots. I did a double take when I saw the empty bed. Samantha and the baby were gone. I peeled off my sodden clothes, put on my pajamas, and padded barefoot back to the lounge.

"Where are they? The Farzads?"

"Oh!" said Izzy. "I was so distracted by your sudden appearance I forgot to tell you. They're gone."

"Gone?"

"The deadling djinn arrived to bear them away. He was extremely grateful."

Typical of a djinn to just leave like that. He was supposed to tell me what he knew about my parents. Wasn't that the deal? Devious djinni. I should have known.

"So ... that's it?"

"He complimented Lou's turning magic."

"I'll pass on the message," I said.

Celestine meowed at the werewolf, who was pacing again, and seemed eager to leave.

"They looked very happy," said Crowe. "The deadlings. A snug little family. You should be pleased."

"I am," I said. "I was just out of my depth. I don't know anything about deadlings, or djinn, for that matter. And my knowledge of birth ... well, I'm just so glad you were here."

"Stop it," said Izzy.

"Stop what?"

"Don't go all soft on me. It's not your style. We're supposed to be arch-enemies, remember?"

The witch winked at me, and her cloak turned from navy to black. It was her StarDust cloak, the one with the effervescent gold stars. She picked up her magical Mary Poppins handbag, and Celestine, whose coat was also fizzing, and made for the door. The werewolf was waiting for her.

"You're leaving?" I asked. "But you said yourself that it's dangerous out there."

"Laurent will accompany me," she said, and I'm not sure if I imagined the gleam in her eye. She obviously liked the idea of being escorted by a werewolf.

"Oh," she said, turning, her cloak swishing around her. "I almost forgot."

"Forgot what?"

"The deadling djinn. Alif? He said I needed to tell you something."

Smoke, like that of what the djinn's clothes were made of, rose in my chest. "Yes?"

"Living between the veils ... he felt the presence of a ghost here, in your home."

I swallowed hard. "Yes?"

"He said the ghost is trying to communicate something to you."

My heart lodged in my throat. "What?" I asked. "Communicate what?"

"He wasn't sure."

It felt as if my brain would explode in frustration. I put my palm on my forehead and closed my eyes.

"That's all he said? What the *faex* am I supposed to do with that?"

Isadora shrugged. "I don't know. Not my circus, not my monkeys."

"Well," I said. "That's helpful."

"He just said you should listen to it. '*Listen to the ghost*,' he said. It's important."

I felt like kicking something. The deadling had been in the best position to find out what the message was. Couldn't he have tried a little harder? Conjured up a little smoky ouija board? Didn't he realize, I fumed, that if I could communicate with the ghost, I would?

I took a deep breath and thanked Isadora. I didn't want to be alone, but I let the witch and the werewolf go. I didn't have a choice. Maybe it was a good thing to have some time to myself. I needed to feed Gizmo, sleep, and plan what to do next. I thought of my haunted fridge and my stomach howled. No groceries, and no chance of buying any, either, because the city was burning and the shops were looted.

As I began to close the door behind Crowe and Laurent, someone else appeared on my doorstep. It was a goblin dressed as a courier delivery man, bearing a fruit basket bigger than his head, which was quite a feat.

"Wrong person," I said, closing the door on him. As hungry as I was, I didn't know anyone who would send me a fruit basket. It was either for someone else, or it was a bomb. Either way, I wasn't interested; I preferred my home-baked granola without the extra crunch of plastic explosive. The shortbread looked especially suspicious, dusted with white powder. Anthrax?

"Jacquelyn Denna Knight?" the goblin said, his words muffled by the door between us. He repeated my name, louder, and I opened the door again and narrowed my eyes at him.

I didn't trust goblins at the best of times. And this was certainly not the best of times.

"Who sent you?" I said.

"Forage Florist," he said. "Dot com."

"I mean, who's the basket from?"

The goblin set it down on the ground and plucked the small white card from a clutch of bananas. I'll give the bomber some credit: they were delicious-looking bananas. The muffins looked good, too, shiny and soft-looking, studded with caramelized pecans. There was even biltong for Gizmo. And the chocolate slab—

"It's from Sugar," he said, reading the card. "Sugar? Must be a nickname. Sugar and—" and then he made the sound of a cat trying to dislodge a furball.

"Holy hex," I said. *Sugar Shagar.*

Shagar Khargol. Matriarch of the Khargol familia; Godfather-cheater; husband-poisoner. At first I thought she was just a particularly unattractive pickle wearing lipstick, but I had totally underestimated the orc. She had single-handedly razed the Realm's political status quo by killing her husband while he slept. I don't think she understood the ramifications of what she had done. She was in love and pregnant with her lover's child, who just happened to be her husband's personal bodyguard. It was the ultimate betrayal. He would have killed her if he had found out; she had just beaten him to it. What she hadn't realized is that with The Godfather gone, the Khargol rule would be overthrown by the opposition: the greasy skinheads who were intent on wrecking the Realm.

I grabbed the card out of the goblin's hands and looked him up and down.

"The city's on the brink of a civil war," I said, suspiciously. "Why are you still working?"

He pointed at his uniform. On his lapel was embroidered: *We Deliver No Matter What.*

When I looked up again, he was pulling a face like a nervous sheep in *Wallace & Gromit.* I think it was supposed to be a smile.

ON THE CARD, scrawled in Shagar's terrible handwriting, it said:

DEAR JACKS

Welcomed our bundle of joy today

Because of U

Enjoy the granola it haz cocosnut

Regards

Sugar, Gnarg, and Baby Jackelin

"CAN YOU SIGN FOR IT?" asked the Goblin.

"Do you have the return address?" I asked.

"Yes, but we aren't allowed to furnish that information."

"But if I wanted to send a message back to her, right now, would I be able to do that?"

His eyebrows shot up. "I don't see why not."

I grabbed his pen and wrote on the back of the card.

DEAR SUGAR

Come back immediately.

Hammerskins are destroying the Realm and killing Khargol loyalists.

You need to fix what you did before it's too late.

I SHOULD HAVE ADDED *Congrats on the cocktail pickle* but I was in a hurry and I ran out of white space. I handed the pen back to the goblin, along with what was left of the envelope of cash I had received from Samantha Farzad at *The Copper Cog,* when she was still alive and pregnant, and the pub was still standing. Then I tore open the clear cellophane of the fruit basket and gathered up a couple of muffins and some fruit, and bundled it into the goblin's arms. He looked puzzled, because no one was ever kind to goblins.

. . .

Sudenly, there was a scent in the air. Copper. Crimson. I reached for my wand just as I saw the swish of a cape in the corner of my eye, but I wasn't wearing my utility belt. I was wearing pajamas: an old, oversized *Rockin' the Realm* T-shirt, and sleep shorts. Was it Demetrius, coming to finish me off? No. There was no crackle of danger in the air.

"Lysander," I said to the blood-scented air. "Long time, no see."

The handsome blond vampire appeared, elegant cape flaring behind him, showing off its beautiful teal underside. The startled goblin almost dropped his bounty. I gestured for him to scamper, and he did.

Lysander and I had a history; a complicated story I'd rather forget. But, like a stubborn case of orc herpes, he kept on coming back.

"I had business to attend to," he said. He picked the fruit basket up off the floor.

"I was wondering about that," I said. "There's been a distinct lack of vampires in my midst recently. I knew it was too good to be true. Knew it wouldn't last."

"We've been … busy," he said.

"That's what worries me," I replied. Now that they had the HighFire Crown, nothing could stop them. We thought the Hammerskin rule was bad, but being under the Silvano Clan would be much, much worse.

I crossed my arms. "What do you want?"

Look, Turkey Bone, I wanted to say. *I've had a long day and I don't need a vampire on my veranda.*

"Why are you here?" I asked. "And don't give me that hurt and offended look."

A shadow scudded over his perfect skin. "I came to warn you," he said.

I sighed. I didn't need any warnings. I already knew how dire my chances were looking.

"You need to get out of the city," he said. "Out of the country."

I laughed. "Well, that would be convenient for you lot, right? No *girl wizards* standing in the way of your clan's plans to take over the Realm."

"Please, Jax," he said. "When you blew up the Venom lab—"

"Who? Me?" I asked, blinking. "What Venom lab?"

Lysander ignored my shoddy attempt at acting innocent. "When you blew up that lab it forced the Clan to think of a new strategy to recruit soldiers. A much more dangerous design."

Filius Canis, I thought. That explosion was one of the few things I had been proud of. I felt chilled and a shiver ran down my spine. I hugged myself, feeling vulnerable without my trench coat on, without my crossbow or wand.

Lysander grabbed my shoulders and looked into my eyes. His were arctic, and mesmerizing.

"Please believe me. Something terrible is going to happen. You have to leave," he said.

I smacked his hands away. "Get off me."

He clenched his jaw. "That's not what you said the other night."

White hot anger flared inside me and the shame flamed my cheeks. That was a low blow, even for a vampire.

"You bastard," I said. "Get out."

"You never invited me in."

I slammed the door and marched to the living room. Then I turned, went back, and grabbed my fruit basket out of his hands, and slammed the door again. Latin curse words exploded in my head as I paced the room. I was so furious I was sure I'd be able to punch a hole in my living room wall. Anger swirled around me like a tornado. As I cried out in frustration, the red hardcover slammed to the floor.

CHAPTER 40
LISTEN TO THE GHOST

isten to the ghost, Alif had said.

I realized then that if there was anyone to be angry with, it was myself. For being TSTL: Too Stupid To Live.

The ghost wasn't saying *Hello* or *Goodnight* or *Make Your Own Bloody Bed Next Time* when he was rearranging my reading material. He wasn't just pushing any book off the shelf. He always moved the red hardcover. The red hardcover. The *faexing* red hardcover!

Feeling like the dumbest wizard ever born, but at the same time excited that I was finally close to working out what the message from my specter was, I grabbed a muffin from the fruit basket and sat down on my charity-shop chair with the red book, and started to read.

The book was titled THE ANCIENT AND SACRED LORE OF VAMPYRES, and had been published long before it became fashionable to put a publishing date in the publication details. Carefully, I turned the first few pages, which were yellowed with age, and the edges were foxed. It smelled of dusty libraries, basements, and toast. It looked like a fascinating book, and I was really interested in reading the whole tome, but right then I wanted to get down to business. I wanted to know what my ghost was trying to tell me.

When I was at the Copperfield Institute, we'd have dozens of books to study, but there was one main book that we studied throughout our time there. It was *The Sorcery Almanac for Witches, Wizards, and Other Magical Creatures*. It was a treasure trove of information, spells, history, and notes on practical and elemental magic. It was common practice during our reading time in hostel, just before lights out, to "let the book choose the lesson." We'd open the book to a random page and that, supposedly, would be the information we were most in need of at that time.

I decided to do the same with the red hardcover. I closed the book, and then opened it again around two-thirds of the way through. What I saw made the hair on the back of my neck stand up. It was the V-Cult killer symbol, the upside-down anarchy sign, a 'V' in a circle, with a double line scratched horizontally through the center.

"What the—?" I said out loud. What was an ancient vampire symbol doing branded on the dead bodies that all bore a striking resemblance to me?

According to the book, the emblem symbolized *The New Dawn*: a prophecy of a future era when vampires would take back their control of the Realm. In order to do this, they'd need three specific magical items. One earth-based, one water, and one air. Together, these fragments would create the fire that was needed to ignite the dawn.

I looked across to my kitchen, which had been swallowed whole by the ravenous plant. The items were not named in the book for safety reasons, but I'd bet my entire fruit basket that The HighFire Crown was first on that list.

These elemental fragments, when brought together, would create a power so intense that it could flatten the entire Realm in an instant. Fueled by this intense black magic, the vampires would be able to create the New Dawn Kingdom, an unshakeable parallel pocket realm, thus rendering the vampires invincible. They would magically summon an Untouched human army, and be able to rule from afar with their iron fists and nasty fangs.

There was even a drawing of The New Dawn Throne, which was a vulgar, revolting thing designed to show contempt for every species. It was to be built with body parts and belongings of magical folk: dead wizards' staffs, witches' wands, elegant elf bones, and gilded with the melted-down gold teeth of dwarfs. The pillow should be orc-skin leather, noted the author, stuffed with werewolf fur. It would be encrusted with the stolen jewels of the fae, and have giant griffin wings attached to the vertical support.

As I looked at the illustration I felt as if my blood was turning black and cold. Something about it seemed inevitable to me, as if I had lived my whole life knowing about it in a small, dark corner of my mind. Fear crumpled my insides as I imagined what life would be like if the prophecy were allowed to come true. I could practically hear the kitchen plant growing along the walls. The dread I felt was pushing me down, forcing me to be small. I had to fight against it, rise above it. I needed to be strong and fierce and bold if I was going to stop the Silvano Clan from claiming the New Dawn Throne.

EPILOGUE

There was a knock on the door. I hoped that it was Darick, although I was pretty sure it was Turkey Bone. This time I would invite him in, I thought, and make him tell me everything he knew about the Silvano Clan, the New Dawn, and Acheron Baldassare. I hesitated, feeling vulnerable in my soft cotton pajamas.

He knocked again and again, making my mind up just to deal with him in said pajamas. I was under no illusions about Lysander: I knew he was an extremely dangerous vampire. Just one look at his carving-knife cheekbones told you all you needed to know. But I also knew, deep-down, that Lysander would never hurt me. I didn't know why.

I wrenched the door open, ready to give him hell about knocking so insistently, when I saw that it wasn't Lysander. It was Captain Musubarin with his shiny new badge and half a dozen Scorpion officers behind him. In that split-second that I gaped at him, he pointed at my wrists, and a neat click sounded. Handcuffs. Another pair appeared on my ankles, and a silver chain reared up like a python and attached the two pairs to each other.

Deodamnatus, I thought. *How many times would he catch me with that handcuff spell?*

"No!" I yelled. "Tilexon. You don't understand." I struggled against the cold metal, desperate to be able to reach my wand and my coat.

He looked so smug in his new uniform and glinting pin. "Really?" he said. "In that case, feel free to explain."

"The vampires," I said. "The Silvanos. We need to work together if we're going to—"

His eyebrows shot up. "The vampires?" he said, mocking me. "Suddenly you're afraid of vampires?"

"You should be, too," I said.

"The *vampires* are being very well-behaved of late," he said. "I have no reason to suspect them of anything. You, on the other hand—"

"Please, Musubarin," I clasped my hands together for added effect. "You don't know what you're doing. We need to find the elemental fragments and stop Acheron before it's too late."

He pulled a strange face, as if I were speaking in tongues, then glanced over his shoulder to address his officers. I didn't recognize any of them. These were all Musubarin's men.

"Search the place," he said. The squad pushed past me and swarmed all over my apartment. With a twist in my gut I realized that I had never destroyed the empty vial of *Spiritus Morbus*. The voodoo serum was a Council-banned substance which automatically got the possessor a one-way ticket to the Black Tower. Terror painted my insides.

"You can't do this without a warrant!" I yelled.

Tilexon snapped his fingers again, and this time there was a bundle of official-looking papers in his hands. He gave me a fake smile so wide you could have played chopsticks on it.

"Not only a warrant to search," he said, "But also an instruction to impound your wand and other magical instruments."

"You wouldn't dare," I said.

"And," he said, enjoying every moment. He licked a finger to help him turn the pages. "A warrant for your arrest."

"*Filius Canis*," I said. "You've got nothing on me."

"Really." He said. It wasn't a question.

"Sir!" shouted someone behind me, making me jolt. I turned to look at the officer. He held up the voodoo vial, and I shut my eyes. "*Spiritus Morbus*," the man said.

"Oh," exclaimed the captain, acting shocked. Then he looked at me, chewing his lip and angling his head. "Doesn't that explain a lot."

I felt like kicking him in the balls again, but thought it might be tricky with the ankle cuffs I was wearing.

"Collect her weapons," he ordered. "Bag them up and take them to the station."

He grabbed one of the officers and motioned at me. "Put her in the car. I'll personally escort her to the Ember Isles."

Adrenaline shot through my body. The fear I had felt just moments ago was back, and the magic was singing underneath my skin. The officer began to lead me away.

"My lawyer is Blimaex Abarim," I said, breathlessly. "He'll explain to you why I have that vial."

"Your lawyer?" scoffed Musubarin. "You've been found in possession of a Council-prohibited substance. You don't get to have a lawyer."

DEAR READER

Holy *faex*, Jax is in for a world of pain.

Are you ready for the next book in the series?

Book 5: The Chaos Jar

Jax makes a bold move, but her actions put the whole Realm at risk.

Also, you won't believe what Sugar Shagar has up her sleeve.

Hope you'll join us on the adventure!

JT Lawrence & MJ Kraus

Also by JT Lawrence

FICTION

WHEN TOMORROW CALLS

• SERIES •

(Futuristic kidnapping thriller)

The Stepford Florist: A Novelette

The Sigma Surrogate

1. Why You Were Taken

2. How We Found You

3. What Have We Done

When Tomorrow Calls Box Set: Books 1 - 3

(complete)

URBAN FANTASY

BLOOD MAGIC

(complete 6-book series)

1. The HighFire Crown

2. The Dream Drinker

3. The Witch Hunter

4. The Ember Isles

5. The Chaos Jar

6. The New Dawn Throne

CURSEBREAKER

(complete 6-book series)

1. The Dusk Reapers

2. The Haunted Portal

3. The EverShade Ring

4. The Obsidian Castle

5. The Pick Pocket's Curse

6. The Eternal Betrayal

STANDALONE NOVELS

The Memory of Water
(steamy psychological thriller)

Grey Magic
(witchy magical realism)

EverDark
(urban fantasy)

SHORT STORY COLLECTIONS

Sticky Fingers

Sticky Fingers 2

Sticky Fingers 3

Sticky Fingers 4

Sticky Fingers 5

Sticky Fingers 6

Sticky Fingers: The Complete Collection:
Books 1 - 6: 72 Short Stories

∼

NON-FICTION

The Underachieving Ovary
(memoir)

The Indie Author Game Plan

∼